forsaken river shore
driftwrack and a johnboat
garden here and there
a house peering out
from the trees on the slope
a new gate bearing an old name —
that of this book PAYNE HOLLOW

PAYNE HOLLOW

life on the fringe of society

HARLAN HUBBARD

GNOMON PRESS

New Edition with Afterword by Don Wallis
first published 1997.

Copyright © 1974 by Harlan Hubbard

Afterword and Publisher's Note
Copyright © 1997 by Gnomon Press

Library of Congress Catalog Card Number:
97-71033

ISBN-10: 0-917788-66-4
ISBN-13: 978-0-917788-66-6

Published by Gnomon Press, P.O. Box 475,
Frankfort, KY 40602-0475

The burning of fire —
Now the blaze increases
as the wood is consumed. This
is the time of greatest heat.
Then the air begins to chill,
we pile on more wood.
It is the rhythm of all things,
The rise and fall of the river,
The pulse of life.

1

This winter evening as I write within the circle of mellow lamplight, the sound of crushing ice comes up from the river as one slowly drifting floe after another rakes along the ridge of piled-up ice which forms the shore. It is an elemental earth-voice, like wind, rain and breaking waves, at once soothing and awful. In an interval of silence I look through the window into the cold, faint light of the young moon which hangs just over the distant ridge of hills beyond the river. It shines on the rippling water between the broad sheets of ice, reminding me of a summer night when the same moon's reflection on the smooth river is shattered by a soft breeze coming out of Payne Hollow. In my mind I can see the rhythmic flashing of many fireflies against the heavy foliage. The earth is good and the changing seasons are a joy.

Across the room, with her own lamp and window, and her own thoughts, Anna is washing the supper dishes. The gentle clatter that drifts over to me does not penetrate my consciousness, for it has long been in the background of my accustomed stint of writing in the half hour just after supper; an arrangement that put to some use this fragment of time at the tag end of the day. With some encouragement I might have dried the dishes; instead, I wrote in the journal.

Keeping a journal is a habit of mine from way back.

It has been done in spurts, however, and often neglected
for long periods. The most lively records were made
during my long canoe trips on the Ohio, when I achieved
as close a communion with the river as I would in later
years on the shantyboat. The shantyboat led to Payne
Hollow, and the beginning of our life here was another
time of near ecstasy. With our minds and hands busy
shaping our new home, the most matter-of-fact entries
in the journal transcended the commonplace and
sometimes contained a gleam of poetry.

Our days in Payne Hollow continued to be so full and
productive, so satisfying, that I desired to write more
about our life here. That is how the idea of writing a book
came about. It aroused my interest at once. In addition
to telling how we settled in Payne Hollow, I could
answer the questions we are often asked—how did you
find Payne Hollow in the first place, what happened to
your shantyboat, why did you choose to live in this
forsaken hollow on the fringe of society? I could describe
our life through the seasons and tell how we sustain
ourselves directly by our own labor, hand to mouth.

I soon learned that writing a book was more
demanding than casual, formless entries in the journal.
Much as there was to write about, it was hard to get
started. I often found myself looking out into the night
or listening to the sounds from Anna's corner. After a
while the writing began to move. I thought about it
when at work outside during the day and those few
minutes after supper became precious. During the

winters I gave some time to writing in the afternoons, usually on the coldest days. I wrote in the house sitting before a window on the upper level, distracted by winter birds outside and warmed by the genial log-burning stove at my back.

A book was taking shape. I kept modifying it, rewriting, supplanting old beginnings with new ones, trying to get to rock bottom. This went on for years, time enough to have written several books. That period after supper was brief, however, the afternoons of writing rare and often the manuscript lay dormant.

We have lived here twenty years now. Tonight I am considering how to end the book, a problem hard to solve while our life at Payne Hollow goes on in full vigor. Perhaps I shall not write a definitive ending, either of the book or of our occupancy of Payne Hollow. It may be written by a bulldozer swooping down to wipe out this remnant of wilderness in the name of progress, or we might simply drift away with the ever passing river, leaving Payne Hollow to work out its future destiny without us. Some memory of our stay here will possibly remain and we may become a legend of Payne Hollow, distorted by time and repetition. In the distant future someone may relate, if anyone will listen to him, how his grandfather, as a small boy, used to go down into Payne Hollow when it was still a wilderness. There on the riverbank, in a house which they had made out of rocks and trees, lived a couple all by themselves. They planted a garden, kept goats, ate weeds and groundhogs

9

and fish from the river, which in those days was full of fish. They never had to go to a store. The man worked with axe and hoe, without machines. He painted pictures of the old steamboats and made drawings of the life they lived.

I am brought back to the present moment by a flourish from Anna's corner as she stows away the pans and closes the cupboard doors.

Now we join in the last scene of the winter day. I roll out a bench before the fire, raise a leaf to form a low table and place our low chairs one on each side. Anna sets up the reading light, a wooden stand holding two ordinary oil lamps, with slanting pieces of aluminum roofing above them to reflect the light downward. One of us prepares to read aloud, the listener gets out some hand work to do. Both reading and work cover a wide range. Some of the books, for we have several going at one time, and some of the chores, last the winter through.

Tonight Anna begins the reading with a few letters from a volume of Brahms–Clara Schumann correspondence. I toast soybeans in a Dutch oven over the coals, an occupation which leaves me free to listen, although the rattling of dry beans might disturb a reader not accustomed to offside noises. After a time we change about, I read from Henry P. Bowie's engaging book on Japanese painting, while Anna works at a heavy boot sock for my use. Knitting is a perfect accompaniment to out-loud reading, causing no distraction to reader or listener, except at points where stitches must be counted.

The fire burns down, the cold comes in closer and sleep hovers before our eyes. We decide to give it up for tonight. The lamp is dismantled and stowed away. The dogs are let out into the snapping cold, to duck quickly into their cozy nests under the house. By a long-practiced routine we slide our bed out of the corner and lower it from a vertical position to a horizontal one. Before falling asleep we watch the firelight and shadow on the familiar beams and boards of the ceiling, the only light now for the moon has set.

About midway in the course of an extremely cold night such as this one I get out of bed to put fresh wood on the fires—in the fireplace near the bed and in the homemade cellar furnace which is reached by a trapdoor and ladder. The fuel is handy and I move in the dark with sureness. After taking a last look at the glittering sky to see how far Orion has progressed toward the western horizon, I get back to bed. The reviving fire crackles a little, the river of ice is still on the move, but no other sounds disturb the silence of the winter night.

When I get up to begin the new day, a faint light shows in the east but the darkness is untarnished. I stir up the fires again and in the flickering light, while Anna sleeps, or pretends to, I crouch by the hearth to cut up some squash and roots for the goats' breakfast.

The stars have lost some of their luster when I go out into the cold and the increasing glow in the east gives distinctness to the bare trees. The stable will be dark, however, so I have lighted the lantern and with this cheerful companion make my way down the icy path.

The kids, who have spent the night in a pen separate from their mothers, begin their piping as soon as they catch a gleam of my lantern. Not yet, little ones, I must get our milk before your turn comes. Here is some hay to hold you over. The little stable seems warm in the lantern's glow, yet you know the morning is a cold one because the goats' hair is fluffed out, giving their faces a strange, round look. The feeding and milking follow an established routine in which the patient animals do their part and I soon leave them to their ruminations.

It is good to be inside the house, which the fires have begun to warm up. Anna has been busy, the bed is made, and together we stand it on end, slide it into its corner. One of the delights of a real cold morning is the wholesome fragrance of cooking cereal. On ordinary days this is done in the fireplace and the aroma goes up the chimney. This morning a fire is burning in the cookstove for extra heat and the cereal is steaming on it, an arrangement which allows the fireplace to burn freely and radiate its heat unhampered.

Breakfast is laid out before the open fire, the dogs having been persuaded to move to another spot, and the meal is followed by the customary bit of reading, preferably from some old book of travel or voyages.

Before engaging in my daily stint of woodcutting I go down to the river shore. The river has fallen to its lowest stage because so many of its sources are frozen. I am able to walk out on the ice which has been stranded on

12

the rock bar at the mouth of the creek, and from its outermost point survey the ice-choked river, upstream to Plowhandle Point and the wide bend beyond, downstream to Saluda Creek and Marble Hill. The whole reach is an arctic expanse. In the whiteness of snow and ice the formal divisions are lost, the river and hills are merged into one element. The small cove above the bar is solid ice bordered by a ridge of slabs piled up by yesterday's wind, along which occurs the crashing and breaking as the river pushes forward its heavy load of ice. Another night like the last one and no sound will come from a motionless, frozen river.

I stop to look at our johnboat lying on the bank just out of the ice. Its side which was exposed to the freezing wind is plated with a row of icicles so perfect and even that they might have been turned out by a machine. The footprints I made yesterday in the soft mud as I worked with lever and tackle to pull the boat out on shore are now frozen hard as concrete.

The old boat looks awkward and out of place there, tilted on the sloping bank. We feel that all is not right when our johnboat is out of water, for then we are mere landsmen. Though not used every day, it requires constant attention. It must be bailed out, tied in closer on a rising river, shoved out when the river falls. It is handy for dipping up a bucketful of water or for washing muddy parsnips. From the house we look down upon it many times a day and we wake to think of it on wild, stormy nights.

What makes the johnboat most dear to us, I suppose, is that it keeps fresh the memory of our shantyboat days of which it is a symbol. We never forget that the shantyboat brought us here, and even though we have taken root on land, the johnboat reminds us that the river is free and long. If some devastating change should come to Payne Hollow—a highway, an industrial plant, the government or bad neighbors, there is always the river, beckoning us downstream to some out-of-the-way bend where nothing would bother us.

Moored in a snug harbor
after a day of drifting, we
prepare for the winter night.

2

Approach an unknown shore in your own boat and even though the place should become your home for years on end it will always retain for you an aura of adventure in a new land, like the freshness of morning remembered through all the day by one who was awake at the dawning.

Our boat was only a homemade shantyboat drifting with the river's current and that first winter's voyage had not taken us beyond the limits of our previous exploration; yet to us it was adventure into an unknown land, for even familiar shores become new and strange when you live on the river in earnest and let it carry you along at its own pace with all the other driftwood. We had to struggle with the river at times and match our feeble strength with winds and eddies. There were difficult landings to make, snags and bridge piers to avoid and countless tows of barges which might run us down. Like the moods of the river, our days might be hard and rough or gentle and easy but none were ordinary or monotonous. Landing at some river town where vestiges of steamboat days were still to be seen, or perhaps only imagined, we went up the muddy bank to the nearest street in search of a store or a source of drinking water, looking about with interest as keen as if we were in a foreign land. Or we might put in at an island

17

or creek mouth to explore, ransacking the drift piles for choice wood and possible treasure. Now and then we tied our boat along some deserted shore for a few days, letting the river go on its way without us.

Toward the end of winter the idea of making an extended layover became more and more attractive. There was not the least reason for shoving on in haste. The river, being of finite length, should always be taken in small amounts to make it last longer. Summer, with its low water and slack current, is no time for drifting, anyway. So, if we could find some rural section of the river that appealed to us, we planned to live there with one foot on shore for a while, for the entire summer perhaps, planting a garden and becoming well acquainted with a bit of new country and with the people who lived there.

We began asking rivermen along the way if they knew of a good shantyboat haven, and were soon told of Payne Hollow. It was on the Kentucky shore not far downstream and seemed to have all that a shantyboater would desire, if for some reason he wanted to be in a quiet place away from towns—a running spring, land for garden, good fishing and an owner known to be tolerant of river people.

On a quiet day of hazy sun—was it winter's end or spring's beginning?—we drifted with the slow current of a falling river down the last stretch to Payne Hollow. We made a landing in a cove just above a small rock bar, moored the boat to a leaning willow, slid out a gangplank and went ashore, alert with expectation.

18

The impatient dogs—Skipper and one of her half-grown pups—did not wait for this formal debarkation but jumped ashore at the first possible moment to disappear yelping into the brush. We were more deliberate in our exploration, sauntering about the sandy bottomland which had been scoured clean by the recent high water, looking up at the steep hillsides where not a green leaf was to be seen on the gray trees. Yet spring was in the mild air warmed by meager sunshine, and swelling buds of soft maple along the creek glowed a dull red. The scent in the air was not of flowers but of sun-warmed slopes and muddy shores, promising fertility and summer growth.

Payne Hollow satisfied us from the beginning and we searched no farther for a summer harbor. Our shantyboat remained at its first mooring, except from some up and down movement in the moderate rises of spring and early summer. The catfish soon began to bite and these served us to make acquaintance with the farm people who lived on the nearest road, a mile back from the river. I often made the steep climb up the stony trail with a sack of catfish, bartering them for milk, eggs, bacon and other country provender. The owner of the land in Payne Hollow, when he learned of his new neighbors, made us welcome. When he planted the small river bottom he left us space for a garden, even breaking the ground one spring day when he was plowing with his team of white horses.

Though our liking for Payne Hollow grew with the

summer, the thought of remaining there never occurred to us. To leave in the fall and continue our voyage down the river was as certain as the departure of the summer birds; yet for one reason or another we tarried at the familiar landing through the shortening days of fall. Winter was at hand when we cast off our shantyboat laden with summer's harvest and drifted away. No one saw us off except old Boss, a native hound who had become a summer friend of our Skipper.

We saw Payne Hollow merge into the endless river shore with no regrets. Our whole interest was in the river ahead, in what was around the next bend and in the river's course far downstream, where the shores and stream itself would be such as we had never seen.

The bayou country of Louisiana—
a strange land to river people,
shores overspread by tropical growth,
strange boats on the water,
shrimp trawlers, pirogues
and pushing skiffs

3

It was in 1947 that we discovered Payne Hollow and
lived there for a long summer. A clean break was made in
the fall, we drifted away with no thought of ever
returning there again. Today we are to be found living in
a house in Payne Hollow and well rooted there. We
vividly remember the shantyboat, but it belongs to the
past.

The way that led us back to Payne Hollow was a long
and roundabout one.

The first leg was the drift down the Ohio and
Mississippi. When New Orleans was reached, instead of
following the precedent established by flatboat men, who
abandoned their heavy craft unsuitable for upstream
work and returned overland to their starting point, we
were so desirous of continuing our shantyboat life that
we turned westward into the bayou country of Louisiana,
the land of the Cajuns. In this maze of connecting
waterways there was no river's current to carry us along,
but we made do with a small fisherman's skiff, a wretched
substitute for drifting. The antique engine in the skiff, a
more likeable contraption than the fussy, high-speed
modern engines, was worn out and gave considerable
trouble. At best it moved our shantyboat so slowly that
the restless dogs sometimes swam ashore to chase a

rabbit they had spotted from the deck; in which case I could pick them up in the johnboat and rowing, easily overhaul the shantyboat before it had proceeded very far.

It was a strange land to river people. The shores between which we sailed seemed about to be overspread by a tropical growth of trees, grass and water-loving plants. Even the air was different, with a new softness and a sea wind. The land near the Gulf of Mexico was a limitless prairie level with the water, where a single distant tree stood out like a ship, and a cluster of live oaks on a shell ridge might have been an island. The canal was a narrow strip of blue water on which the tugboats, towing the strings of barges behind them, sailed straight away until they vanished in the far horizon. The separation of land and water lost its distinctness. Sky became the main feature of the landscape. People were rarely met, but the passing of tugs and fishing boats, and at night the burning flares of oil rigs were constant reminders that we had not left the world of men.

Northward, away from the Gulf the land became higher and at a certain point—a few inches made the difference—a forest belt appeared, almost closing off the sky with overhanging branches and streamers of moss. Farther along were fields and perhaps an old plantation with a decaying mansion and nearby rows of mean dwellings where slaves once lived. If you followed up the bayou it became a small river with a steady current and the slight beginnings of hills and valleys.

On the Intracoastal Canal westward we came to one

bayou after another, their southward course leading to the Gulf. There was much diversity in them and each offered a unique temptation to linger. Bayou Barataria, closest to New Orleans, was a picturesque nest of cabins and small boats, fishermen's docks and stores. Bayou Perot, the next one, was primeval, its untouched shores empty as the sky. Bayou Lafourche was perhaps the heart of the Cajun land. It seemed thickly inhabited because the small farmhouses were all closely spaced along the bayou, the farms being narrow strips of land extending back to the never-distant marsh. There were small towns and bridges, roads, shipyards in miniature and nearer the Gulf we saw many trawlers.

On Bayou Chêne our station was near a roadless community, the barest suggestion of a town, two or three dwellings, a tiny store and a church, backed by the marshy forest. Trade came to the store in pirogues, "pushin' skiffs" and fishing boats. The storekeeper brought in his supplies by a motor boat, the same one that went for the priest every other Sunday. On school days it carried the bayou children to the road's end where they were picked up by a school bus.

Bayou Têche, more than all the others, appealed to the imagination. The old aristocracy still lingered there, and traces of its elegant past. One could believe the romantic legends connected with it. Steamboats once ran on Bayou Têche, also on Lafourche. The only sternwheeler we saw was a gas-driven one, the *Mary-Joan*, which sometimes towed a barge loaded with shells. It was operated by a Cajun family and the children waved every time they passed.

All the people living in the bayou country are Cajuns, descendents of the Acadian French who settled here after their expulsion from Canada, or they had become so by association or marriage. We met them everywhere. Many lived on campboats, the bayou version of the Ohio River houseboat or shantyboat. They were farmers on Bayou Lafourche, planters on Têche and ranchers in the prairies. They trapped in the marsh, manned the fishing and shrimp boats, tended the innumerable bridges that had to be opened to pass our shantyboat through and they worked in the oil fields, shipyards and stores. They had wonderful French names and spoke a baffling patois. We found them friendly, pleasant and helpful. On long stops away from town, the wandering shantyboat was accepted by the whole neighborhood and good friends were made, especially among the Cajun boys. They were curious about how we lived, where we came from and what it was like on the Ohio River. We in turn learned much about Cajun ways and local customs, how to find turtle eggs and how to catch soft-shelled crabs.

In remote places there were older people, the only true Cajuns nowadays, who were suspicious of the "foreigners" from the outside. They could not understand my innocent habits of making sketches of fishing boats, docks, bridges and buildings, of riding about on a bicycle, of asking questions everywhere. This was evidence enough for the Gulf fishermen, who had been alerted by the Coast Guard during the war, and they were sure that at last they had discovered a spy. When state and local police questioned us, they soon convinced themselves of the harmless nature of our background and activities. This allayed all suspicion and we were allowed to merge into the waterfront. This happened at Delcambre. As a final proof of our acceptance I was invited by the tender of the railroad bridge to go up to the top of the tower with him so that I could enjoy the view from the highest point for miles around.

The natural connection of Delcambre with the Gulf was a winding thread of a bayou but this had been widened into a canal on which the white shrimp trawlers were constantly coming and going. By way of the same canal we had arrived at Delcambre well into our second year in Louisiana. Our future course, which had of late been uncertain, now became clear: we would not pass another winter in the south, but would return to the Ohio River. The decision to leave this seductive land and the waterways which beckoned us westward had been hard to make. Worst of all would be to abandon the shantyboat, but this we were resigned to, having convinced ourselves that towing it back that long distance against the awesome current of the Mississippi was not practical.

Delcambre, a thoroughly Cajun town, with many small boats in its narrow harbor, was a fitting place to end a bayou cruise. Before settling down there we explored a lake reached by an extension of the canal. On its shore was a salt mine, one of the "domes" found in Louisiana, the source of Jefferson Island salt, a name familiar to us because it used to be painted in large letters on Kentucky barns. Joseph Jefferson, the famous actor, once owned the lake and built a castle which is still on its shore.

It was a pleasant, shady place and we might have remained there for the rest of our time had it not seemed more sensible to be near town where the sale of our fleet could be promoted. We put up a sign "Campboat for Sale" on the highway, and began a general overhauling of everything on board.

Being within a town was a novelty after the many lonely stations in marsh and forest. From our windows the people and their activities in the outer fringe of cottages could be observed and some of our neighbors visited us. A closer acquaintance with Delcambre revealed strange undercurrents in its society, and questions were raised which would require a long sojourn to answer.

The sale of our outfit proceeded slowly, or not at all, even though we made our best efforts, spreading the word everywhere and advertising in the newspaper of a nearby town. I scouted the flat country by bicycle, discovering unsuspected waterways used by trappers, stopping at country stores and following up any lead, much as I disliked the business. To ride through the new country with nothing on my mind would have been more enjoyable.

A young trapper working in a liquor store by the bridge during the summer showed an interest in the campboat, but was evasive. We heard at second hand of his boast that he would wait and buy us out for next to nothing. This desperate climax was averted by the offer of a rancher to buy the whole fleet—campboat, motor skiff, Ohio River johnboat and everything that we could not take with us. His marshy ranch being intersected by unbridged creeks, he planned to remove the cabin and make a barge of the shantyboat hull for transporting cattle and farm machinery. It seemed a mean and dismal fate for the beloved little ship, but after some reflection we thought it better than falling into unappreciative and careless hands. We were consoled also by the attitude of the rancher's wife, who would make use of everything —the cookstove, Anna's stock of canning jars, even the cupboards and drawers, the doors and windows. No doubt the heavy anchor found a place on some fishing boat.

How to get ourselves, the two dogs and all our traps back to the Ohio River was a problem that had been on our minds ever since the boat was put up for sale. Now it had to be decided. Ownership of an automobile went against the grain, but that is what we came to—a bulging old Dodge, not in very good condition; yet it served us well, though retaining some of its weaknesses to the end. To complete the equipage I constructed a folding camp trailer. Its chassis was a two-wheeled boat trailer, made of iron pipe by a local welder. With a few cypress boards and large panels we fashioned a flat box ten feet long that could be opened and expanded into comfortable sleeping quarters, somewhat restricted but well protected from the weather. Compartments were worked into the box to accommodate gear for cooking along the road, food, water, camp chairs and all essentials. There was a cargo space in the hold. Of course the car was crammed full, but everything had its place. Skipper, a fastidious dog, objected to sharing the back seat with her overgrown pup, Sambo, so she rode in the front between us. The cello, in a handmade trunk, stood in the back, wedged between floor and roof.

To build and arrange all this was the work of many days in the hot June sun, but all was ready when our last day on the shantyboat arrived. It was a Sunday. The whole fleet was headed down the canal, making slower progress than usual against the tide. The new owner guided us into a narrow creek, so narrow that the shantyboat had to be helped around the sharp bends by a pole. Arriving at the ranch, we moored the shantyboat for the last time and left it on that nameless stream.

The rancher's wife invited us to dinner, which was an excellent one, cooked and served in true Cajun style. As we lingered for a few words on the veranda and looked over the green, shimmering landscape, it occurred to us that this was the sort of place we were seeking, remote and timeless, beyond the reach of highways, beyond today.

Our old landing, when we got back there, was so empty and desolate that we quickly drove away, taking the northward road.

As we returned from Louisiana
the Ohio River lay before us
like the Promised Land.

4

It was a strange predicament for a pair of shantyboaters
to find themselves in, adrift on the highway, spending
money every day, flowing with the stream of traffic
through one town after another, crossing bridges over
rivers whose names, if they could be learned, meant little
to us. To give up close communion with the green earth
and quiet waterways where solitude and silence were
normal, and the ample days were measured by the slow
progress of the sun across the sky, for the hardness and
dissipation of the restless world of the highway was a bad
bargain; yet we rolled along in good spirits, even joyfully
and without looking back, being strengthened by a
conviction amounting to faith that our shantyboat life
need not come to an end even though we had lost our
boat. The shantyboat spirit would prevail in whatever
circumstance. Even such a routine and prescribed
business as traveling in an automobile was redeemed by
our unique outfit with its homemade touches, by our slow
and halting progress from one real camp to another along
back roads and rivers.

Back roads and rivers have attracted me for as long as
I can remember. I have avoided highways and towns
from a sort of instinct. This was strengthened into a firm
conviction that the accepted ways, not only of traveling,

but of living and getting a living were not for me. To engage in the world's work would be mortally difficult, and the world's rewards were not worth the price I would have to pay for them. Somehow an abiding love of the earth became part of my nature when I was quite young and I went on from there. When I began to paint, I turned without hesitation to the landscape I knew and loved so well, particularly to the Ohio River. I had dabbled in the river all my life, camping, canoeing, tramping along its bank, associating with river people, fascinated by steamboats from the very beginning.

To achieve more perfect harmony with the river and at the same time to live close to the earth and free from entanglement with this modern urban world, I became a shantyboater. Although this was a natural consequence, it came about surprisingly late in my life. I was old enough to be called middle-aged before I ceased being a dilettante and took to the river in earnest.

I was just as slow about taking a wife, a step which had been made difficult, almost impossible, by those vague longings of mine for an idyllic life in nature. I had discerned that marriage and becoming a respectable, contributing member of society were closely allied and I had realized that I could make a go of neither. Still, it is a mystery how entanglement of some sort was avoided.

At length I found a way out through Anna. She was not at all a shantyboat type and she had no river in her upbringing. Indeed, she had scarcely taken a good look at the Ohio River, though librarian in a river city for some

34

years, until I introduced her to it. She was town bred, to all appearances of a conservative mind, with high standards of respectability and cleanliness, the least likely person to accept a rough life on the muddy river; yet she showed no hesitation. In fact, she encouraged the immediate undertaking of the shantyboat venture after I had told her of my leanings in that direction.

It turned out to be not such a rough life after all, and the river was not always muddy. The roughest was at the beginning when we lived in a shack on the riverbank put together of odd boards and tar paper, material which later went into the cabin of the shantyboat. Yet we never had happier days, and under Anna's management the shack became an inviting, cozy dwelling. The boat when completed was a marvel of neatness and comfort. Though bare and without ornament, like a Japanese house, its cabin seemed spacious, having a pair of large, sliding windows on each side and an open fireplace. It was efficient, too, with a place for such uncompromising articles as Anna's cello and a beehive. Regardless of these departures from tradition it was a real shantyboat, undeniably homemade, rough, an unwieldy affair to handle, sturdy as a barge, able to withstand hard knocks and the battering of the elements.

Not only the shantyboat and the shack on the riverbank, but everything we were to do together, derived vitality and significance from this combination of roughness and refinement, a result of the tension between our contrasting natures; yet beneath the surface and never disturbed was an underlying ground of sympathy between us which reconciled our diversity.

Speeding northward in our glass and steel capsule we felt like disembodied spirits scouring the earth on a quest perhaps hopeless. The automobile is an epitome of modern civilization—it promises much but conceals fatal defects. We grudgingly made use of it but were not taken in by its blandishments. The shantyboat had set us free.

We expected to come down to earth after our arrival at our home port on the Ohio River, but the far-ranging automobile prompted us to further extravagances. "Why not," it said, "since you have a tested vehicle and camper, explore other parts of the country? A region yet unknown to you, wilder and not so worn as the Ohio valley, might be more favorable for you to make a new beginning in and regain the freedom and sense of completeness enjoyed in your shantyboat life."

Little persuasion was needed. After unloading all surplus cargo and rearranging everything else more efficiently, we again took to the open road (a jesting misnomer for today's highways) and headed west, toward deserts and mountains beyond the horizon, and the blue Pacific.

Camp in the desert
under a wayside paloverde tree

5

A country never before seen, new roads to follow, cooking fires along the way and camp beds where all was unfamiliar except the stars, and unrecognizable sounds came from the darkness; camps by rivers and mountain brooks, in the desert high and low, by the ocean's shore; strange birds to be seen everywhere and a new book to learn them by. Best of all was the freedom to go in any direction, to linger as long as we wanted. This was traveling of a high order, even if it depended on an automobile, which is too exacting for such close association, always demanding something; yet viewed more simply, the car and trailer together formed an admirable contraption, being in the nature of a shantyboat, at once conveyance and home. It allowed us to take along all sorts of things—books, painting material, tools, extra clothes, a hand grist mill to grind flour for journey bread and a Dutch oven to bake it in. What other manner of traveling, unless it were in a gypsy cart, would allow an impromptu duet of violin and cello under a wayside paloverde tree?

We are conscientious travelers, observant and alert in a new country. The spectacular landscape of the West, the true wilderness, the vast openness of the land, made the Ohio River country seem insignificant and monotonous, worked out and worn, a region of mist and half light, its river polluted by many cities. For all this, we were not tempted to abandon it. Our roots had gone deep into that alluvial soil and we had lived there in happiness and contentment. It was our home and possibly we were too old to accept another.

At any rate, by the following spring we had swung around and were headed back to the East.

Each section of the country we passed through on our eastward journey had a spring season peculiar to itself— the desert in flower, the soft, moist warmth of the Gulf Coast, planting time in the red soil of Tennessee. It was still early spring when we reached the Ohio River where the pale, misty sun and chill air brought the season into focus for us.

Although this was the lower part of the river, far downstream from our home port, we hopefully took up the search for a likely place to stake a claim, exploring all promising bends and reaches, going out of our way to visit certain spots which had taken our fancy on the downstream voyage five years before. This meant working our trailer in and out of narrow lanes, over stony roads and steep hills, but the results were not worth the trouble. We learned again that all places when approached from the land side lose the charm they had for the river voyager, to whom everything appears in harmony with the river landscape. To him the modern world seems to have vanished and he would not be surprised to see teams and wagons waiting on the grade as an old steamer sounds its landing whistle.

Some locations we had been hopeful about were altered beyond recognition by a new highway or vast industrial plant. It was not only the physical presence of these intruders that spoiled the country for our purposes but they seemed to have caused the neighborhood to deteriorate. The country people were giving up farm work and were driving long distances to jobs in the new plants. Prosperity had made them expect easy gains, it had disturbed old customs toward strangers. Distrust had taken the place of honest curiosity and our innocent mission was misunderstood.

Yet untouched areas remained, lonely bottoms with old farms and sandy roads, abandoned hamlets where a few people lived in the ruins, content with the river and hills.

Once we almost found what we wanted. An old man lived alone in an old house on a river ridge from which fields and woods sloped down to an empty farmhouse in the bottom. It was a place of peace, away from the stream of progress, for the road did not follow the river around this bend. The old man was friendly and hospitable but his married children did not approve of his welcome to wandering strangers.

We kept poking about in likely lanes and landings but discovered nothing that could hold us. The disparity between the free earth and the tight parceling out of all the land was discouraging. Months of camping along the road had led us, like the gypsies, to think lightly of fences and ownership but insuperable difficulties arose when it came to finding a corner where we could stay for good. Something was wrong. Were we trying to force the issue? Somewhere the right location was waiting and in good time we would come upon it.

It was one of the many strange processions
down the Payne Hollow road

6

Returning from the western excursion we found ourselves
back at our base camp on the Ohio River, which had been
the point of departure for our shantyboat venture nearly
eight years before. We were not at all happy about being
there as our "base camp" was a suburban house, the sort
of place we were determined to keep away from. The
house had its good points however, and many old
associations. I had built it years ago as a home for my
mother, and we had lived there more or less happily until
her death, which befell in the year of my marriage to
Anna. The house then became ours, but with no hesitation
we abandoned it and went down to the riverbank. There
we began to build the shantyboat, happy to escape from
the house, the support of which would have taken all our
efforts.

At present we were thankful to have it as a place of
refuge. During our wander years the house had been
rented and by now the tenants were good and faithful
friends. Our coming back need not disturb them, as we
settled ourselves for the time in a small building well
down among the trees in the back yard which I had built
years ago as a painting studio. A solid, harmonious
structure of salvaged brick, timber and stone with a slate
roof, it was good to enter it again. The one room seemed

spacious after the trailer camp, though it offered no more
in the way of conveniences. We felt secure there, sheltered
from the surrounding world. The large window was some
compensation for not being in the open country because
it looked down a wild ravine too steep for the building of
more houses.

All of a sudden it occurred to us that we might stay
right here and live with contentment for an indefinite
period. The ravine offered a secret escape to the river and
fields. At night the distant lights of the city suggested
advantages lacking in the wilderness—concerts, museums,
libraries, friends with whom to converse and make music.
I could clear again the old garden spot farther down the
hill. Beyond was park land—but no, these allurements
had lost their power over us. We could not live in town
again or become part of the sterile closed-circuit world of
today. The shantyboat and our nomadic life had opened
new ways which we must follow.

Often when driving a monotonous stretch of highway
on our recent travels, I had dreamed of the quiet and
lonely life we might find in some back country beyond
the road's end, long ago abandoned or passed over by the
expanding world, a second-growth wilderness where
undisturbed we could participate in a celebration of the
earth and its seasons. On a hillside slanting to a friendly
river we would build a rude cabin of stone and hewn
timbers, so close to the shore that the breaking waves
could be heard within doors. The woods and river would
supply fuel for the hearth and food for our table. We

The dogs caught a groundhog, Jess gave us catfish from his net, there was an abundance of poke greens and ground nuts. We had the first swim of the year in the muddy water. Even so, there was not enough to hold us there and we went on up the river.

Change was everywhere. A new highway, scarring the hillsides and desecrating the lonely valleys would soon be extended all along the Kentucky side of the river. The new high level dams under construction would make the river a series of long, bankfull lakes. The old dams, low and movable, were bad enough, but they allowed the river to be itself for much of the year, and we had adjusted to them. Progress was inevitable, however, and the new conditions would bring more city people to the river towns, more pleasure boats to the river. This was not at all what we were searching for. We gave up, crossed to the right bank on a gas-driven ferry, one of the few left of any kind, and retreated down the highway, bidding farewell to the ghosts of the past.

Our next sortie was to Michigan, Anna's family home. It was new country for me, and I felt closer to wilderness there. For our purposes two drawbacks were evident: a long cold winter, and vacationers everywhere. The Ohio River appeals to us because it has no attraction for outsiders. As for winter, we enjoy it, and the year would not be complete without a winter which was long and severe enough to be genuine. That offered by the Ohio River latitude is usually satisfactory on all counts, although deep and lasting snows are rare. An advantage is in the amount of firewood needed here, which is considerably less than in Michigan—a meaningful difference when you cut the wood yourself by hand. Also, the Kentucky growing season is some weeks longer at each end, a boon to those who live directly from the land and aim to have a year-round garden.

Toward the end of May we could think of nothing better to do than revisit Payne Hollow. During our five years' absence Anna had corresponded with Aunt Maud McMahan, thus keeping in touch with Trimble County friends. It would be nice to see them again. Before leaving town we got the little canoe out of the loft of George's garage, where it had been dreaming for a long spell of years. Inverted on the trailer top it rode very well and added a new touch; perhaps it foretold our return to the river.

Our initial voyage to Payne Hollow in the shantyboat had taken most of the winter. Now, five years later, we drove there in three hours, but it wasn't the same place. The Payne Hollow we arrived at, after so many experiences on the river, could not be reached by automobile.

We were in familiar territory now and the farms were known to us by name. We pulled up at Owen Hammon's house, where the old Payne's Landing road begins. Owen came sauntering out, smiling as always, and greeted us "Hi, Harlan" in an offhand way as if he had seen us yesterday instead of five years ago.

This was the way Trimble County welcomed us back.

50

Enough of that day remained for a walk down to the river, accompanied by Skipper and Sambo, our shantyboat dogs. Mother Skipper might have memories of Payne Hollow, but Sambo had been born far down the river.

As we began the descent, everything was just as we remembered it, the trees arching overhead, the source of the creek, the sandstone ledges and the cedars fragrant in the warm sun. The stony road slanted down the hillside, and turned right to keep an easy grade. Here we left it to follow the steep shortcut path down into the triangular field where the old stone chimney stood like a monument. Beyond the field the hollow narrowed and then opened out into the diminutive bottomland. Now we could see the riverbank trees, the river itself, all unchanged. Friendly as it was, the place had the wildness of remote hollows and deserted shores where people might once have lived, but now were long gone and forgotten. No trace of our summer's stay could be found, the garden spot was overgrown with weeds and heavy brush. Yet we were happy to be in Payne Hollow again and our shantyboat life there seemed more real than our recent trip over the highways. We had a swim off the bar, admiring anew the splendid vista up and down the long reaches of river. We drank from the spring where it ran from under the rock ledge at the very bottom of the creek, the same nettles stinging us as we climbed up the muddy bank.

That evening we set up camp in a pasture on the ridge close to a tall cedar, or juniper, which had a deeply indented, angular silhouette like a Japanese drawing of a pine tree. Owen came by, said he thought that with a tractor he could drag our trailer down into Payne Hollow, if we wanted to camp near the river, promising to come around next "evening," meaning sometime after midday, when the last of the tobacco plants had been set out.

He appeared in due time, not alone but followed by his entire family, also by a neighbor and his boys and of course a string of dogs, everyone interested and ready with friendly help. Owen drove the tractor, the neighbor and I steadied the trailer over the rough places, Anna and Daisy talked together, children and dogs whooped and dashed about. It was one of the many strange processions that must have gone down the Payne Hollow road to the river.

We followed the road around the long way, made the hairpin turn, forded the creek twice, the end of the trailer dragging, through the field and past the chimney to the narrow part of the hollow where it was near to the creek and shady all day, handy to river and spring. The trailer was left in the middle of the road, the only opening among the elms and sycamores. Our escort went back up the hill and we were left alone in Payne Hollow.

Cut into the ramparts of the hills
along the Ohio River are many notches
that mark the outfall of small streams...
The distinctive feature about Payne Hollow is
the way it has been cut through the long bluff that
walls the eastern side of the river at this point.

7

Cut into the ramparts of the hills along the Ohio River
are many notches which mark the outfall of small
streams, some of them narrow and steep-sided with just
room at the bottom for the rocky creek bed; others more
open have gentle slopes, farmhouses along a winding road
and water in the creek pools even in dry seasons. They
are so similar that only a devoted and long-experienced
steamboat pilot could keep track of all these hollows and
creeks, their order and their names, but he would know
each one and could tell you a story about it, and who
lived there; for the mouth of each little valley is someone's
landing. This feat of memory was made easier by the fact
that each opening in the hills had some noticeable
peculiarity to set it apart, a conspicuous landmark, the
way the river curved at that point, the formation of the
hills, an island, a sand bar. Some of their names have a
touch of poetry: Big Bone, Stepstone, Bullskin and Cold
Friday, but most are merely descriptive—Notch Creek,
Crooked Creek and Straight, Red Oak, Corn Creek,
Grassy and Brush. Where the creek does not amount to
much, the notch takes its name from the hollow, like
Payne Hollow. The Payne who gave his name to this
particular notch is unknown in this generation. No one

can remember farther back than the time when Payne Hollow was part of Norfolk Plantation, belonging to the Prestons, the only slaveowners in these parts. The next gap downstream from Payne's is Preston Hollow, above which on the ridge the old plantation house is still standing and is still lived in.

The distinctive feature about Payne Hollow is the way it has been cut through the long bluff, about 450 feet high, which walls the eastern side of the river at this point. The slope upward from the river is so steep that the customary willows can find no foothold at its base. Forest trees grow from the water line to the top where sheer rock appears, with a fringe of cedars against the sky.

Although the creek which comes down through the hollow is never called Payne's Creek, it deserves a name, since it is more than a rocky watercourse to carry off the rains. It comes from quite far back in the folded hills and approaching the river winds through a miniature bottom. At the creek mouth is a rock bar thrust out into the river by runouts strong enough to roll stones. The narrow bottomland extends up and down the river for short distances to taper off into the bluffs.

Payne Hollow seems never to have had many inhabitants at any time. Perhaps the Indians could not feel secure in this narrow valley hemmed round by wooded slopes. At any rate, few traces of them have been found here. Nor was there room for ambitious farmers. It takes another breed to work these irregular patches of bottomland, to clear and plant hillsides; men whose nature leads them to the fringe of society, to marginal lands where they are less under the eyes of their neighbors. Only two small farmsteads were established in Payne Hollow. One was back from the river in the level opening between two forks of the creek. The other was at the base of the river bluff, not far below the creek. The spring in the creek supplied their water, but it must have been a tricky climb with a full bucket when the bank was muddy. Even a moderate rise of the river drowns out the spring. This was only one of the many tribulations these people had to put up with, and they gave it up at last, moving to a place on the ridge road. House and barn were carried away by the 1937 flood. Now it is difficult to find the neatly-laid stone foundation among the trees and undergrowth, more difficult to imagine that the house once stood in the open with an unobstructed view of the river, except for two huge weeping willows which screened the western sun. The nearby root cellar, however, is intact and ready for use. The low entrance looks like a natural cave in the hillside, and if one ventures inside he finds an ingeniously constructed dome of plastered stonework, a circular concrete shelf near the floor and a hole in top for ventilation.

All that remains of the other house, the one up the hollow, is the stone chimney and fireplace. It was standing firm when we first came to Payne Hollow, but later the upper half toppled over in a winter storm. This must have been a lonely place to live, closed in by hills, with not even a glimpse of the river except in high water, only the sky for outlook. The tale of a murder committed there, the prime legend of Payne Hollow, might have been invented by a lively imagination under the spell of this secluded place, but it really happened. By this time details of the affair have grown hazy but from what we have heard a woman was involved, the daughter or sister of the man living in the lonely house up the hollow. The lady had a friend who persisted in crossing the river to see her, in spite of warnings to keep away. On one of these visits the Payne Hollow man shot and killed him. For this deed he served a term in the penitentiary, but returned to these parts and continued his work as farmhand. The house was never occupied after the shooting. It might have been carried away by the great flood of 1937, at the crest of which, according to the old hunter, only the top of the stone chimney was above water.

In the pathless woods you sometimes come upon sites of more primitive dwellings where no one remembers a house to have been, marked only by a heap of stones that was once a chimney, or by a mortarless wall around a spring which no longer flows. Stories are told of hunters, herb gatherers, moonshiners and mussel fishers whose rude shelters of driftwood boards and old canvas have long since gone down the river.

Payne Hollow reached its high point in steamboat days. From Payne's Landing a road led inland winding along the creek which it forded three times before angling up a hillside to the farm country above. The road was well kept and much used by farmers to reach the river and the steamboats which were the only direct connection between country and city. A small shed and corral had been built near the landing to hold the freight and livestock awaiting shipment on the next boat. There might be cows, calves, lambs and pigs, usually footloose and herded with difficulty up the gangplank. The passing boats often picked up crates of chickens and a tale is told of a flock of turkeys that was driven down to the landing for shipment to the city market. According to the season boats were loaded with tobacco in hogsheads, eggs, peaches, apples, grain, potatoes, fresh vegetables and hay. On the return trip they brought all manner of stuff from the city to the farmers. Even the big mail boats would stop at Payne's Landing, their pilots always on the alert for a signal to land—a shout or waving, at night a bonfire or a burning brand tossed into the air, a swinging lantern. It must have been a sight to see those towering sidewheelers nose into the bank to the accompaniment of jangling bells, escaping steam, creaking blocks, shouts of men, mooing cattle.

Most of the Payne Hollow freight was handled by small local packets, a long series of them over the years, not steamers toward the end but gasoline-powered sternwheelers. No scrap of business was too small—a pilot claims that he was once hailed into shore by a farmer who wanted change for a fifty-cent piece. These boats were often patronized by housewives going to town on a shopping trip, for they could return in the evening on the same boat with loaded baskets and shopping bags.

These diminutive packets with their explosive engines continued, for some years after steamboating had died, to serve this section of the river, where the steep shores, the "Narrers," delayed the construction of a road. Often the boat was built by the owner at his riverbank farm, with the helping hands of his boys and kinfolk, and the crew would be a family group. Every detail of the shores and their inhabitants, down to the dogs, was known to them, every aspect of the river—ice, flood, low water and wind. Wind waves on the long reaches, as in the case of a south wind at Payne's Landing, could be a danger to those small boats when loaded to the guards, or at least the women passengers thought so; no disasters are recorded, however.

The *Revonah* and *New Hanover*, the *Dove*, *Bedford* and *Hattie Brown*, all of them are remembered with affection, and with a feeling of loss, by everyone who knew them. With their passing, Payne Hollow's mild prosperity came to an end. The road was neglected; the fields, unsuited to mechanized farming, became sproutlands. The great flood swept away all traces of habitation, the narrow, offside valley was deserted. Anna and I were attracted by the very conditions which caused it to be abandoned. We are unique among its inhabitants, not farmers, nor fishermen nor shantyboaters in the accepted sense; yet closer to the earth than any of them, with true respect for the river and the soil, and for Payne Hollow. May it long remain as it is, not merely for our selfish enjoyment, but for the satisfaction it must give many people to know there is such a place. Few wild pockets are left along the river these days.

The homesteader

8

From the first our shady camp by the creek seemed like
the end of the road. This was partly because the
automobile, which meant moving on, had been left at the
top of the hill. It had never been a congenial companion,
and here it would have been thoroughly out of place and
intolerable.

Camp began to have a settled look when a bench with
a back to lean against was constructed of stray boards
between two small elms. A wooden box found among the
driftwood and nailed to a tree made a handy cupboard.
The canoe was launched at once and as we paddled the
nimble, responsive craft, skimming lightly over the water,
we became aware of a grace that had been lacking in our
shantyboat years. The next step was to set a trotline out
in the river. To carry the stone anchor in that narrow,
round-bottomed canoe and heave it overboard at the end
of the line without mishap was a feat requiring delicate
balance. We baited the line every day about sunset and
traced it early the following morning. June, supposed to
be a good fishing month, came up to expectations. We
ate catfish every day and soon had to provide a live box,
made from a stranded barrel, for the surplus. I took a
sackful up the hill now and then for our fish-hungry
friends, who no doubt had been hopefully waiting. The
milk and eggs, or possibly a chicken which I brought

back in exchange, or an invitation to help ourselves to cherries and strawberries were most welcome to the squatters under the hill.

Sometimes Anna and I would go together on these bartering excursions, or we would make a foray into town. Returning laden with store-bought foods or country produce, our spirits rose as the road and houses were left behind and we descended the leafy trail to our green solitude.

Days and nights there were full of wonder, even the commonest and most often repeated workings of nature acquired a deeper meaning. Part of this must have been due to the exuberance of June. It began at daybreak with the chirping and chattering of birds close at hand and in widening circles around us. And then, what greater wonder than the rising of the sun? Even the nights, as yet without insect choirs, were alive. Fireflies against the mass of trees across the creek were flashing galaxies which repeatedly made and unmade abstract patterns of light, voiceless as the stars overhead. The deep silence might be disturbed by a bird for whom the night lasted too long, often a chat, whose series of unrelated squawks, grotesque by day, against the nocturnal setting became a weird unearthly chant of great beauty.

The days were busy ones. We could not resist planting a few garden seeds around the edge of a patch of late corn in the Payne Hollow bottom, hoping that the yield would at least compensate for the purslane and lamb's-quarters which had been plowed up for the corn. I took my painting equipment to the old barn up the hollow, where I fitted out a studio almost in the open air, setting up one of the unhinged doors for an easel. A shortage of strawberry pickers on the hill gave us a chance to be helpful, to earn a little and to indulge our fondness for this finest of berries. Anna canned them, also the wild raspberries near the old farmstead across the creek. The raspberries must have been cultivated there originally and some were of a rare yellow color. Later we picked gallons of dewberries and blackberries in the abandoned upland fields and pastures. Our precious stock of canned stuff was stored in the old root cellar, after I had made a door to keep out possible marauders. Later canning of tomatoes, peaches and pears just about filled the circular shelf. To have put the root cellar into service again gave us much satisfaction.

As the heat of the sun increased, the canopy of trees became an important feature of our camp. The hot weather brought on thunderstorms, often at night, and we lay in our low bed listening with apprehension to the roar of water dashing down the creek.

One tranquil evening when paddling in to our landing after baiting the trotline, we noticed a man sitting on a log, apparently waiting for us. He stood up as we came near and Anna recognized him as Jesse, the hunter, a frequent visitor in shantyboat days. It was he who had introduced us to Payne Hollow.

"Heard you had come back," he said, "just wanted to welcome you home."

His remark touched us, but it had little to do with our deciding to remain in Payne Hollow, except that it brought to the surface an idea we both had in our minds: Payne Hollow was certainly the place for us, having everything we desired. It was unoccupied, we were here; why not stay?

Our first impulse was to pick out the most suitable location, gather up stone and timber and start building a shelter for ourselves. The chances were that no one would have objected, but then we recalled our recent wandering among strangers, how homeless we felt, confined to the narrow strip of road, with someone else's land on both sides. This still seems an unnatural practice, but since it is so firmly established, we thought it best to subscribe, although our intention was not to keep Payne Hollow all to ourselves.

The land here had changed hands during our five-year absence but it was still owned by a friend. Even so, we had prepared ourselves for a refusal and were delighted when our proposition was favorably received. Yes, he would sell us a strip of land in Payne Hollow, but not until the government had made up its mind. We learned that the purchase of an immense tract of land in these parts was under consideration and Payne Hollow might be swallowed up.

In the face of this uncertainty we went ahead and tackled the first and most important problem: where to put our house. We scrambled about on all possible sites, trying to imagine a house here or there and what living in it would be like. Although the only habitation in the hollow close to the river had been south of the creek, we chose the north side because it was fully exposed to the sun. The snow never lay there long nor were the cold winds severely felt, according to our hunter friend, who knew the hollow in all seasons.

So our house would straddle the ridge formed by the intersection of the slope from the river with that from the creek. It would face southwest and have a fine view of the river. From the beginning we had determined it should be above flood level, although construction would have been easier lower down on the natural terrace where our shantyboat garden had been planted. Since no one could inform us how high the 1937 flood had risen on our hillside, we did some rough measuring. By means of a carpenter's square, a piece of string with a weight on one end and a tape line we were able to calculate approximately the elevation of our chosen site above the normal pool of the river. It appeared to be safely above the highest flood crest. The Ohio is never expected to exceed this mark and we hope this is a true prediction, but for our part, flood water in the cellar would be a small price to pay for the sight of the river grown to enormous size, extending from our hill to those on the far side, covering the tallest trees.

In September the news came that the government had gone elsewhere to purchase its land. To us this was a cause for rejoicing, although the blow would fall elsewhere if not here. Be that as it may, we were pleased that Payne

Hollow had been saved and that we could establish ourselves here. The possibility of being forced to give it up had made us realize how much we wanted to stay.

A deed giving title to the land must be forthcoming. For some reason, possibly because we were here and had the time, the writing of the deed fell to our lot. Knowing almost nothing of such matters, we were forced to rely on the deed of the farm from which our plot was to be taken. We were to have a strip on the upstream end, beginning at the river, crossing the narrow bottom, up the slope and down the other side to the creek, whose winding course completed our boundary. The old deed was a quaint document, giving the measurements in poles and referring to boundary marks impossible to locate, being trees that had disappeared or stones not distinguishable from their fellow stones. Timely assistance came from a man who had once lived on the farm above. He pointed out some rusty fragments of barbed wire buried deep under the bark of trees, assuring us that this was the line fence. It looked the part, for the trees there were larger and older than those on either side where the ground had been plowed. Cultivation seemed impossible because of the steepness, but our informant said he had raised crops there, and he was a man whose word could not be questioned.

We made an attempt to measure the boundary line, up from the river and down to the creek, scrambling and sliding over rocks and through greenbrier thickets, holding the tapeline as nearly level as possible, for you are not to measure along the slope. The figure arrived at did not tally with that on the deed, but we did not press the point. Better one error than two.

When our new deed to "seven acres more or less" was finished it was accepted by all parties without question. Naturally its style was that of the old deeds, and its matter was similar even to the point of designating an impermanent boundary marker. In our case it was the big double cottonwood at the mouth of the creek, which toppled into the river and floated away within a few years. The mouth of the creek is still in the same location.

Now that the way was clear we set about the actual putting up of our house with much eagerness. We gave all possible time to it, working as long as the light lasted, for the shorter days and cool October nights reminded us that the season was advancing toward winter and the hours were more precious than ever.

Had there been unlimited time, and a virgin forest to draw upon, we might have built our house entirely with materials at hand—logs, hewn timbers, stone, earth and straw. With conditions as they were, however, it seemed more sensible, if less poetic, to use sawn boards and scantlings in part, always making as much use as possible of the trees and stones on our hillside, and of the river drift. In any house which a civilized man would build for himself, whether he be transcendental poet or shantyboater, the use of some prefabricated material— glass and nails for instance—can hardly be avoided; though I suppose he could get along without anything of the kind, to prove a point.

For our boards and 2x4s we went to a local sawmill. It was operated almost entirely by one man who bought a few trees from local farmers here and there, cut them down and hauled them to his saw. Without hesitation he promised to get a load of lumber down to us in Payne Hollow, a place he knew from "forty years ago." Old-timers have often used this figure, probably because it was forty years ago that Payne Hollow was abandoned. The trip was made without incident, but when the truck started down the hill, the lumberman's helper preferred to get off and walk.

We could not have procured a more satisfactory lot of wood to build with if we had cut and sawn the trees ourselves. All of it was rough, of varying widths and thicknesses, and of different kinds, being mostly red oak, ash and poplar, but many other trees were represented— walnut, wild cherry, cottonwood, linden, beech, hard maple and some I did not know. Its variety stimulated inventiveness in a way that a uniform lot of machine-perfect stuff never could. Since not even a logger's truck could get up to our building site I had to pack it up the last fifty feet. This was a good way to learn the weight of unseasoned lumber.

I love wood, and therefore took great delight in our treasure, studying each board as I handled it, assigning it to the best use. I wished again for time to build in a more deliberate manner, fitting the boards and timbers carefully and fastening them with wooden pins instead of spikes.

70

Our mode of construction was that of a barn: a stout framework of posts, not sunk in the ground but based on flat stones, with diagonal braces at the corners; the posts carrying horizontal beams on which the ceiling joists rest, also the outside ends of the rafters. A low stone wall supported back ends of the floor joists. In front they were so high above the ground because of the slope of the hill, that a timber was notched into the corner posts to hold the floor joists in a level position.

Two layers of siding were put on, with building paper between for insulation. The inside boards were diagonal, so that no other braces were needed; the outer ones vertical with battens over the cracks. These boards were not stained or painted but left to weather into the beautiful gray of an old barn. I used galvanized nails to avoid rust streaks, but the streaks might have added to the picturesque effect. The ceiling was formed of wide cottonwood boards which could be removed in summer for coolness and ventilation through the large window in the gable.

Although the construction was simple, it proceeded slowly. To work on the rough hillside was awkward, stones must be gathered up, everything was heavy, the wood was hard. The posts and beams of locust were cut on the hillside above the house and dragged down. An apparently straight tree is remarkably crooked when lying on the ground. We made use of some quite wavy timbers for floor joists to save going farther for straighter ones, and they served very well when one surface was hewn as nearly straight as possible. The hewing was done with a heavy broadaxe, a precious relic loaned to us by Mr. Mac, with steel so hard it rang like a bell. Handsome young sycamore trees with the bark left on made the ceiling joists. As these had to be dragged uphill from the creek bed, we made more concessions in the matter of straightness.

It was a satisfaction to work with poles and rough-hewn timbers. They came direct from the living forest, while boards cut by a saw are dead things.

October is likely to be a dry month, but on a few days rain interfered with outside work. Then our refuge was the unused tobacco barn farther up the hollow. A cooking fire was made on the dirt floor and while Anna prepared our midday meal I worked on the new johnboat. This project was almost as urgent as the house, for the little canoe was a summer craft only, not equal to the drift-laden and treacherous currents of the winter river. Also the johnboat was needed to ferry building material and supplies across the river, an easier way than toting it all down the road from the top of the hill. After some searching about in sawmills and lumber yards I had found a good "pattern" (a country name for the boards to be used in building a new johnboat) of cypress in sixteen-foot lengths. The traditional Ohio River design, with broad beam and square ends, could not be improved on, but I hoped that the fine lines and graceful rake of our boat would set it apart from the slab-sided boxes so often used by fishermen. Owen hauled the boards down to the barn,

which easily housed the boat-building operation along
with the rainy-day camp and my painting studio. It was
a cheerful place. Smoke from our fire curled up among the
barn timbers and tier poles to the roof high overhead
where rain pattered unceasingly. Underfoot, Skipper's
latest puppies played about on the littered floor.

To be building a house and a boat at the same time
was almost too much. Either one would be occupation
enough, not only as to time and energy, but in both cases
imagination and inspiration are essential, and much
deliberation.

My hammering in the hollow barn sounds loud
over the countryside.
It reaches the ears of busy men here and there,
they say, what is that? or
Harlan's working on his boat this morning, or
have the Hubbards begun their house?
That pounding seems to come from Payne Hollow.
Some think to themselves —
that nail went wrong,
he hit the wood that time.

Now I am silent, writing this,
but soon will send more reverberations
in all directions,
across the river, into the hollows,
over fields to the tops of the hills
and into the sky.

As the evenings in camp became cooler, sometimes frosty, our defenses against the night breeze down the hollow had to be strengthened. At first it was warm enough in the lee of the trailer, with a campfire burning. We soon closed up the gap between the trailer and the ground, then placed the engine hood of an old truck behind the fire to reflect the heat. A canopy overhead came next and eventually the sides were closed with canvas. This made a cozy shelter in which we could eat supper and read a little by our hurricane lamp, a gallon jar with a candle inside, before crawling into the trailer bed.

All possible time was given to the new construction. It was no sacrifice to give up our former schedule which had allowed some reading, painting and such amenities as could be practiced in a November camp, because nothing is more exciting than to build your own house. On the twelfth of the month it was possible to move from camp into the bare, raw structure that would in time become our home. We left the little trailer, which had served us well for a year and four months, with some regret, for we knew that years might pass before we could enjoy a nomad life. The change was made less drastic by moving most of the trailer into the empty house with us. The bed, being a flat box containing air mattresses, was lifted out, carried up the hill and set up in one corner on temporary legs. The boxes which made up the kitchen part of the trailer served the same purpose in the house. We brought in also the two low chairs used on our wayfaring. This worn camp furniture gave a homely air to our new quarters. The fireplace, too, was much like the campfire along the creek. The same old truck hood formed its back and sides and a few creek stones made a hearth. Some time in the future we would build a permanent fireplace of stone, but this one would do for the present, both for heat and cooking.

The metal fireplace reminded us of the one on the shantyboat, and the single room was about the same size as the shantyboat cabin, the house being twelve by sixteen feet, the boat cabin ten by sixteen.

These old ties were comforting but the house was to be more than a continuation of former ways. It was a new departure. We looked forward to fresh experiences and to growth into something we were not before. Who knows what can develop, if time and place are right?

Our buildings in Payne Hollow —
house in center, goat stable on left,
shed-workshop on right.
　　Looking north from creek bottom.
River off to the left.

9

In leafy summer the house in Payne Hollow is likely to be missed by a river traveler, although a habitation of some sort is indicated by a johnboat, a fishbox and an assortment of river plunder scattered about the shore. Only from one point, a little way downstream, can the house be seen through a gap in the trees. Even this one opening would have been closed by the fast-growing cottonwoods had they not been regularly topped, a job which is easiest to do from a johnboat on a fairly high stage of water. In recent years, however, the caving banks have removed just about all the shoreline trees. Even so, the house remains nearly concealed by a second defense of trees farther back from the river.

If the traveler should land in the cove above the rocky bar and climb the bank on a series of random planks so steeply placed that toe cleats had to be nailed to them, he would see the house not far above, peering out from the trees, so firmly planted on the hillside that it seems to have grown there. The long roof lines continue the slope with an upward thrust and a window, tall and wide, reflects the blue sky, in contrast to the warmth of weathered boards and the stone foundation underneath.

From the riverbank a haphazard path leads up toward the house. After crossing the narrow, sandy bottom it rises by a few stones to a narrow shelf which was once the Payne Hollow road, then up another bank and through a slanting garden. Off to the left at the edge of the woods is the goat stable, a sort of fairy-tale structure overtopped by a giant hackberry tree, from whose roots a little bridge gives entrance to the loft over the stable. If the goats are at home, one or another of them is always to be seen contemplating the world from this bridge.

The path now climbs more steeply to reach a small flagstone terrace at the left of the house, a point where the average visitor is willing to stop and catch his breath. The terrace is shaded by trees but has a view of the river downstream and, in the foreground, of the small bottomland, a garden in the summer. Beyond are the close-standing trees along the encircling creek.

Four broad stone steps lead to the house door, a solid barricade with a handmade latch. Within, the large window is still the dominating feature. Its lower part is made up of four glass doors opening on an outside deck. This deck is supported only by extensions of the unhewn poles which are the floor joists. The top of the window is higher than the ceiling, part of which is removed in summer to reveal the entire window and the rafters above. Opposite the window the stonework of fireplace and chimney rises through the center of the house. All is open, no inside walls divide the space into separate rooms.

The interior is made even more informal by two levels of floor which are connected by three steps alongside the chimney. A unified effect is given to the whole by wooden walls, ceiling and floors, but this is by no means monotonous for the different kinds of wood vary in grain and color, and in texture as well; some boards having been left rough as they came from the saw, some partly planed with saw marks still showing. A table of walnut, with old electric pole cross-arms for legs, is smoothly finished, and so are the wide ash boards which are the tops of the ledges under the windows. The floor is of sycamore, an unusual wood for that purpose. It serves well, however, because one of its virtues is a grain that does not raise or splinter. The wide boards are of differing widths and the surface has a handmade unevenness.

A stranger upon entering sees only a "living room." It can on occasion be kitchen, dining room and bedroom; also a laundry in winter. It is sometimes a temporary workshop and I once made an extra large painting there. All the gear needed for the various activities is kept out of sight by the walnut paneling, and the wood-burning cookstove hides modestly in the stonework of the fireplace.

On one side of the large window are bookshelves of cherry wood and in the corner next to it is a large panel crossed by strips of cherry. This seems to be part of the wall, but it is a shallow box standing on end, having within it a mattress and bedding, held in place by two removable strips. All this is unseen until the box is slid out of its corner. For use as a bed it is lowered to a horizontal position, one end supported by folding legs, the other resting on a bench which has several other functions.

On the other side of the window, taking up nearly all that end of the room, is the venerable piano, a Steinway grand which has long been Anna's pride. Massive, black and ornate, it is out of character with the rest of the interior, yet strangely it seems to belong there. Like everything else in the house, the piano is given constant use and loving care. Every day its rich tones fill the hollow to the brim and reach the far shore through open windows.

A thoughtful reader will begin to think that this house has a degree of refinement, even a certain naive elegance, that he would not have expected to find in a riverbank cabin erected as their home by two ex-shantyboaters who were seeking to live close to the earth.

I myself am sometimes troubled by this same question. What has become of the one-room shack of boards resembling a cabin in Appalachia that we built in Payne Hollow?

These reflections, and my writing as well, were interrupted by a fading of the light. The winter nightfall was approaching and certain chores had to be done.

Each time I step out of the house, how great a revelation it is! One forgets, even in a brief interval indoors, what it is like outside in the life-giving winter air. You must rise to meet it. You are inspired by earth and sky, seen so many times, yet ever new and unknown.

The sun was about to set on this February day, its level rays were reddening the crest of the eastern ridge. Below, Payne Hollow already lay in the shadow of night. From its depths rose the sound of running water, different voices coming from here and there as the creek flowed in its uneven course over the stones.

After the hour of writing it was good to have some hand work to do, something which went along quickly without much thought or attention. I split into kindling a straight-grained block of driftwood pine, using a dull hand axe, a good tool for this trifling job. It bothered my conscience a little to burn a piece of wood so full of potential use; yet the pine was so perfect for kindling in Anna's stove, the block such a pleasure to split, releasing its fragrance, that perhaps this was its best use after all.

When the woodbox had been filled with some of the kindling and heavier locust already cut, I went down to the river's edge where the johnboat lay half asleep on the quiet backwater. Outside the line of trees the full current of the river sped silently along, bearing incongruous masses of driftwood. This was shantyboat river and my spirits rose at the sight of it. I was overcome by the old feeling of isolation, of sweet and comforting aloneness that used to accompany a winter nightfall when we lived afloat. Away from the river, I knew, was the turmoil of a busy world of people, flashing lights and roaring wheels, but all this had no reality here. I rejoiced that I could live so completely in nature. True, a diesel towboat or a plane flying overhead might break the spell, but these would soon pass into the night and the balance would be restored. Even the worst of conditions could not destroy my vision.

The river had begun to fall. I shoved the johnboat out into the deeper water and tied it, stern to a branch just above the water, bow to a fence post. My jump to solid ground pushed the boat well out from the present shoreline. I watched it swing into position and come to rest, ready for what the night might bring.

My round led me next to the goat stable, where the little band was watching me approach, impassive and silent as if speculating on my intentions, though they knew them right well. The stable was dark inside, the goats filed in following their invariable order, the first one pausing at the threshold, one forefoot raised, to peer suspiciously into the corners. I fed them grain and hay, took what milk was coming to us, and this rite finished went up the stony path to the house. Its angular silhouette stood out against the radiance of the rising moon and from a window shone the warm light of lamp and flickering firelight. Picking up some firewood, I went within to enjoy the special pleasures of evening.

In due time we were seated before the fire on low chairs which allow an intimacy with the blaze—not the same chairs, but patterned after the shantyboat ones, and made of cherry wood. Lighted candles and the simple food our supper consisted of were arranged between us with the care and thoughtfulness that Anna gives to every meal. The silence of night was but little disturbed by our fragmentary conversation, given as it is to long pauses in which only the fire is heard. Our conversation might be compared to the fire, at times going forward briskly, then subsiding into glowing embers. Sometimes it must be poked into life. Our truest communion and understanding is attained with only a few words between periods of communicative silence.

Now my thoughts returned to what I had written about our house in the afternoon of this day. I asked Anna if our life in Payne Hollow was becoming more refined and complicated—or did I use the term "civilized." We could agree that our building a house and living here had not hindered Payne Hollow's reversion to wildness, a trend which had begun when the farmers abandoned it. The effects of my woodcutting and gardening would soon be obliterated if I were to desist. No devastation of wilderness need be feared from a man using only hand tools. The riverbank is just the same as it would be if we were not here, its form and surface molded by the forces of erosion and silting, by current, waves and summer growth.

After a pause, Anna answered, "Our house is larger now, but it hasn't changed."

This seemed at first an evasive statement, without much significance, but after turning it over in my mind I could see the truth of it. Although our house is more than double the size of the original cabin, its character is unchanged. The same construction and materials have been used, no partitions divide the space. We still use oil lamps, burn wood fires, have no store furniture, curtains or decorating. The metal fireplace has given way to one of stone, a second bed stands up against the wall out of the way, just as the first one did. They are much like the bed on the shantyboat. We do have running water, at the cost of building a cistern and buying a small gasoline-driven pump to transfer the water to a concrete tank above the house; a concession to mechanization which has allowed Anna to use water freely without thinking of the toil of carrying it from the spring or river—and I am relieved of the toil, though I still carry water for the goats, partly to indulge in the pleasure of dipping clear water from the river, or preferably from the flowing creek. The burden of carrying has been lightened by a neck yoke. I made one very quickly as an experiment and it worked well. Another, improved in design, as I thought, was not successful. Discovering that a yoke imported from Germany was available, I invested two dollars to see what a real one was like. It was almost identical with the first one I had made.

The carrying yoke appeals to my imagination more than the motor pump, of which I am somewhat ashamed; but surely I may be forgiven this weakness, and not be accused of abandoning former ideals.

Yet I must admit that our house in Payne Hollow has developed into something not intended.

In my old dreams of a wild existence on the riverbank, the shelter I would build of unhewn timbers and hillside stones would be a dark, smoky cavern with an earth floor, like the habitations of the pioneers. The cabin in Payne Hollow as it was when we first began to live in it offered only the bare essentials—shelter, windows for light, a place to build a fire, yet even then it was not the earthy hut I had dreamed of. A woman's influence was already manifest. It became more so as the house expanded until a degree of refinement and even elegance has been attained that I would not have thought possible without the sacrifice of simplicity and honesty. This is all to Anna's credit, though how it was brought about I do not know—nor do I think she does. At any rate it is an achievement to be proud of.

I sometimes regret that my old longing to live closer to the earth can never be fulfilled, but our life together has been richer, more satisfying and productive, than my solitary one would ever have been. Of this I am sure.

Alone in the woods
closed in by dark
trees and snow
with axe and saw
chopping sawing
splitting his thoughts
which he will bring home
in billets on his wheelbarrow

10

This February morning, as on nearly every winter day, and always with unfailing eagerness, I climb the steep hillside which rises above the house, carrying axe and saw. On the way I pass stumps cut in former winters, those near the bottom already decaying, since they were the first to fall.

My chopping and sawing has altered the character of this hillside noticeably. In the beginning we burned only dead wood. Very little can now be found. When I began to cut living trees for firewood, the least desirable went first; then larger, straighter ones where they stood too close, leaving the finest specimens to adorn the valley. With the trees thinned out, more sunlight reaches the ground, causing the disappearance of flowers and plants which thrive best in shade and moist leaf cover. Even the wild larkspur and blue-eyed Mary, which once covered large areas, are about gone. Instead, the wild grass is springing up, and the goats have good browsing on this south exposure in the earliest spring. Woodcutting benefits them directly in winter, too, for they relish the buds, twigs and bark, especially of the topmost branches of the newly felled trees.

It was surprising to find such a heavy growth here when we took over because much cutting had been done on this slope through the years, and part of it was cropland not so long ago. Some of the remaining trees are immense—red oak, chestnut oak, ash, elm and pignut. Locust was most sought by the farmers for fence posts and by ourselves because of its fuel value, yet a good stand of it is still there. Hackberry furnishes most of our firewood. Some farmers have no use for it, but we find it very satisfactory in both fireplace and heating stove. It is a white, straight-grained wood, easy to saw and split, and it has the virtue of burning well when green. I have cut some of all kinds that grow here, even red bud and ailanthus. All have their use, and the less desirable kinds increase in value when brought in. What a beautiful fire some worthless looking, half decayed stump will make!

In years of cutting I have worked over the whole slope. Fortunately there is a narrow shelf on a level with the house, a natural for a wheelbarrow path, and of course for a footpath, too. After the more accessible wood was hauled in, I extended the track around the shoulder of the hill to the eastern slope, bridging a gully on the way. It was a long trip home, pushing a wheelbarrow load of wood, but up to a certain point it was easier than getting the wood down from far up on the hill. That point has been reached and now I am working up near the top, cutting the wood into pieces that can be tossed down to the wheelbarrow path.

Just getting up here with your tools is something of a struggle. Wet or dry it is a slippery climb, and the problem of non-skid shoes is yet unsolved. I pause to look down on the river stretching off into the blue distance. The receding shores and the Payne Hollow slopes make a pattern of angles with the level horizon, against which rise the bare trees. The view up the hollow is closed in by woods, with a foreground of tall, white sycamores along the creek. As no house, barn or road can be seen, it has a wilderness look, especially in snow.

The wilderness spell is deepened by the coarse rasping of the saw, the CHOK CHOK of the axe. These are noble tools and they belong to the woods. What tool is more simple and efficient than the axe, a perfect example of functional beauty. My one-man saw, which was old when it made the shantyboat voyage, is still in service. For this heavy cutting in Payne Hollow I bought another one, similar but longer with larger teeth. To my dismay, some of its teeth were broken off by the butt of a tree which slipped off its stump to the ground, barely missing my toes. To replace it I tried a two-man saw five feet long, which someone had given me—remembering Willie Fitt on the Mississippi River, whom we saw standing in a johnboat sawing a floating log with such a saw, minus one handle. It might cut through a half rotten "blue" log, but I found it too limber for my sawing. Thereupon I converted it into an oversize bow saw by arching a piece of plastic pipe from one end to the other, having removed both handles. This proved to be an efficient saw and I have used it for several winters.

To saw easily and quickly one must keep his tools in first-class condition. The teeth of a saw must be not only sharp but carefully jointed and set. The raker teeth must be just the right length; that is, not quite as long as the cutting teeth. A saw much used needs frequent adjusting and sharpening. This saves time and makes a pleasant job of one that is plain drudgery with a dull saw; yet even though I know this well, I am likely to postpone the sharpening of it, waiting for a rainy day.

Wedges and maul are seldom used because wood that is hard to split is left in chunks for back logs in the fireplace. A wedge is often useful to drive into the cut behind the saw, so that the cut will not close and bind the blade. For this purpose I use a small, pocket-size wedge which is really a brickmason's blocking chisel, having a wide, wedge-shaped blade and round handle, all made of one piece of steel.

Some of the trees I fell are quite large, for this region, and one does not rush into cutting a two-foot butt by himself. He studies the tree again and again and when at last his mind is made up, the time must be just right and the saw in first-class condition. Trees which grow on a slope nearly all lean downhill, more or less, and this gives you an advantage. You start sawing on the upper side, of course, and it is slow work at first. When the cut is deep enough, it is opened a little by the leverage of the treetop's weight and then you have it made. The saw cuts faster, soon there is an ominous crack. You pull away from the tree but nothing happens. More sawing, and more. Time now to get safely away. Slowly at first the top swings toward the earth. The lumberman sings out TIMBER, always a near ecstatic cry, even for an old hand. A heavy tree will crash through everything, a lighter one often lodges in the branches of standing trees. You finally get it down to earth, after making several cuts in an awkward position, or perhaps you are obliged to fell other trees to clear the first one. Trees, even small ones, are always so much larger than you expected when they are stretched out horizontally.

Several sessions may be required to cut up a large tree into firewood lengths. I work up even the small branches; twigs the farmer would call them. They make good fuel, and not so much litter is left in the woods. After a stint of sawing and chopping comes the game of tossing the cut wood down to the wheelbarrow track. You try to get each piece as far down as possible on a throw. The branches often slide quite a ways, heavier sections will roll. If a short piece of the trunk is turned loose it will quickly gain speed, rolling faster and faster. I watch it. There it strikes a tree and is deflected. Now it will stop, I say to myself hopefully. No, it slowly rolls a few more turns, goes over a root and is put on a straight course again. Faster it goes until it spins vertically, making great downward leaps and cartwheels. It is bound to go all the way down to the creek now. Of a sudden it strikes a large tree head on with a loud wooden thud and stops dead. I keep count of those which roll down into the creek and carry them back up to the wheelbarrow track, lest a runout in the creek wash them away. Not being a gambler, I usually split the heavy round sections into halves before starting them down the hill, but even some of these run wild.

Weather seldom interferes with my getting in wood, and well that it does not, since there is never much of a reserve on hand. I do not go along with those farsighted people who cut their winter's wood in summer. That would be unseasonable, like gardening in winter. Working with axe and saw can be enjoyed only in cold weather. It matters little how cold it gets. On zero days when a rough wind blows from the northwest I retreat to a sheltered spot on an easterly slope where it is so warm and balmy in the sun that I shed my outer jacket. In deep snow a path is soon beaten down and I cut the trees near it, which have been reserved for the occasion. Rain is bad. I give up then and work at my bench, or just stay indoors with Anna and enjoy the warmth and burning of the fires.

The wheelbarrow is my year-round cart. It has a box for hauling soil and compost, a rack for grass and leaves. For firewood only the chassis is used. It is a bony skeleton of rived oak, asymmetric, yet well balanced. The thickness of the rubber-tired wheel suggests a wooden wheel.

Though most of our firewood comes from the hillside above the house, there are other sources and wheelbarrow tracks leading to them. My choice of the place to cut wood on a particular day depends on temperature, wind, mud, snow, ice or the kind of wood needed; whether it be hard wood for cold weather, green wood for long lasting fires, stove wood or light dry stuff for starting fires; or my whim at the moment might send me off in an unreasonable direction. One path goes down the "new road," a trail to the creek which I cut out of the bank when getting up stone for the foundation. Another goes along the stony slope facing the river out toward the "Hall place," where some later-day pioneering was done. Sometimes I go across the lower garden, if it isn't too muddy, and through a gate into Newt's pasture, a small area bounded by the creek where I once tried with no success at all to pen up a very active buck goat who had other ideas.

A part of our fuel is river driftwood, mostly willow, cottonwood and the like, good only for quick fires in spring and fall. In low water I sort through the tangled masses which build up against the trees when the river is up and am sometimes rewarded with an oak plank, a locust fence post, perhaps a chestnut fence rail or a piece of white birch down from the mountains. Red cedar is to be found, too, and black walnut, with the white sapwood all worn away. I often go after firewood in the johnboat on a rising river. The shores are not muddy then, and woods beyond the wheelbarrow's range are accessible. Just at the crest of the last rise I made an upstream expedition, advancing easily in the backwater but pulling hard around flooded trees and packed driftwood, just inching past the branch tips swayed by the rippling water as it shot past at a rate which seemed beyond the power of arms and oars to overcome. After a landing in a

93

promising cove the dogs leaped off eagerly, as if it were virgin territory and not just part of their daily run. For me the novelty was to be cutting where the trees were not all known and marked, where dead trees and fallen branches were everywhere. Soon the johnboat was filled with all sorts of wood, light and heavy, some boards and slabs, a stump or two, leaving just room to work the oars. The dogs found an uneasy footing on top and we shoved out through a screen of branches, to be seized by the current and carried away with the speed and quietness at which I never cease to wonder. During those few minutes of drifting I was lifted out of present circumstances. I became a voyager passing strange shores. Payne Hollow was just another place along the way, to be viewed and speculated upon. Yet I did not go beyond our landing. A few strokes of the oars brought the boat in, the dogs jumped off and I tossed the cargo of wood out on the shore. I shoved a wheelbarrow load as I went up to the house, following an easy grade, part of which is an incline of planks carefully lined up. From the top I looked down on the river and saw it again with my everyday eyes. It was still racing past the outer trees, and nothing was on its surface except a few snags and mats of trash.

Whenever I lift axe and saw from their pegs in the breezeway the dogs appear at once and joyfully bound off ahead of me when I take up the wheelbarrow handles and indicate a course. My spirits rise too when we set off. The practical business of getting fuel has been transcended.

To me the winter would be well spent if I did nothing but gather wood to burn in an open fire, where I could watch its sublimation into smoke and ashes.

The house in Payne Hollow. Winter.

11

In the milder days at the end of February my zeal for
cutting wood begins to slacken. I figure there might be
enough on hand to last through the inevitable cold spells
of spring. At least I can now cut smaller trees and easy
wood like box elder and soft maple. The big saw will
probably not have to be filed again.

In the woods, where on winter days only the passing
notes of the bluebird could be heard, the chickadee now
begins to whistle his four-note song of spring and the
titmouse loudly repeats his single note. Suddenly I hear
the first phoebe, his thin, rasping voice in keeping with
the pale sunshine. As I pick up my axe (its handle
marked with a red band lest it get lost in the snow or
fallen leaves) I notice a new growth of tiny green shoots,
and here and there are the first blades of squaw corn,
which will enliven our end-of-winter salads. The flower
buds atop the elm which I have just cut down are
beginning to open, and they will be salad for the goats,
who will not fail to find them. All at once I am overcome
by the thought that the time is spring. When did it
begin? Who saw the very first redness on the soft maples?
The buds on the branches of the cottonwoods that trailed
in the swift current were swollen and shiny, suggesting
candle flames. It is exciting to think of the changes soon

to come to the barren and lifeless earth. This hillside will burst into greenness, the trees will close in the earth with a canopy of leaves.

Always, however, along with this exultation at the coming of spring is the remembrance of winter, an enduring time, stark and simple, when change almost comes to a stand. Yet one cannot cling to what is past. The present moment is too urgent.

This year
his garden
will be
the best ever—

12

In winter, woodcutting; in summer, gardening. Our
calendar is never so precisely divided, for cookwood must
be rustled up in summer and the garden is a year-round
concern.

All our living is regulated by the revolving seasons.
They determine what we do, what we think and talk
about, what we eat, the pattern of each day. Our house
adjusts to the seasons, opening in the summer and closing
against the winter's cold. The time of our getting up in
the morning depends on when the sun rises. Who would
want to lie abed in a summer dawn, when the air is filled
with birdsong? On the other hand, there is not much use
getting up in the dark, even during the shortest days of
winter; yet I often do so, assisted in extending the day
by a late-rising moon, which furnishes light enough for
woodcutting, even when it shines through a layer of
cloud. It is never so dark that my feet cannot find their
way on known paths. Firewood or something is always
waiting to be carried up the hill. I can grind flour by
touch. A lantern provides enough light for many other
jobs—threshing beans, cracking nuts, sharpening an axe.
The hungry goats do not mind being waked up, fed and
milked at an early hour. Writing goes well, close to a

stove where a little fire burns; or I just sit there in that brief period of detachment between night and day, my thoughts following strange paths unknown to sleep or waking.

Sometimes the dark becomes wearisome, I feel my loneliness and look in vain for the faintest glow in the eastern sky or for a lighted window across the river. When at last the strengthening light brings release it seems to promise fair and untried fields of action. All too soon the colors of dawn fade and the familiar world reveals itself.

March, not January, is the two-faced month, for its weather can be that of winter or spring. In our calendar the balance swings from woodcutting to gardening in March. There come a few warm, balmy days when fires are allowed to die and a tantalizing smell of spring is in the air. I take a favorite hoe from its winter resting place and go down into what was last year's garden.

The appearance of the lower bottom, where the main garden will be, is very discouraging, even on a sunny day in early spring. It may be covered by the backwater of a late winter flood; or the water may have receded leaving a plain of soft mud which the summer sun will bake into a bricklike crust, a sore trial for a singlehanded gardener with a hoe; or it may be half covered by flotsam left after a rise which was not high enough to carry away the mats of branches, grass and weed stalks with seeds by the millions, along with trash from the civilized world. The most conspicuous item in these later days is a scatter of

102

plastic containers of many colors. At least they do not break and cut the bare feet of the tiller of the soil.

It is a fortunate circumstance that we have higher ground for early planting. I turn my attention to this and make tentative scratchings here and there, working out some sort of pattern. An advantage of hand tools is that small, irregular plots can be laid out. The driest soil can be planted first; the parsnips still in the ground, the sprouting daffodils, parsley and comfrey can be skipped over. I decide that the early potatoes will go in there, at the top where the drainage is good. A short row of lettuce and radishes here will be handy to the path, and Anna's herbs can be planted behind them. I lay out a large area for spinach, which ranks high with us, both fresh and canned. That must be planted soon.

The very beginning is perhaps the best part of a garden. Now the breeze feels as soft and sweet as it used to on the first spring day that I could go barefoot. The whistle of a cardinal comes from far off through the hazy air. The sun, riding higher in the sky, arouses not only the buds and seeds but also the dormant hopes of the gardener. The memory of past mistakes and failure has been washed out by winter rain. This year his garden will be the best ever.

Encouragement is needed at this point. The bare and empty space to be planted looks immense. However, I know from past experience that the task is not insuperable. A bountiful garden and one fairly well taken care of can be achieved without extra help, without machinery and without chemicals. I have long practiced minimum tillage. Mulching is helpful but it does not save labor if all the mulching material has to be rounded up by means of a scythe, rake and wheelbarrow. A permanent mulch is out of the question on the lower bottom where it would be floated away nearly every winter by high water. On higher ground an over-winter mulch is a hindrance because it keeps the soil cold and wet, thus delaying the early plantings which are necessary to get some crops matured before the hot summer sets in. We have made our gardening easier by eliminating some troublesome and redundant vegetables, like broccoli and cauliflower. Asparagus, rhubarb and comfrey, coming on year after year of their own accord are a boon, as are the never-failing wild crops which need only to be gathered, such as pokeweed, nettles and dandelion. Many more are offered than we now make use of because, having labored to produce the garden crops, we eat them first.

One feature which makes our gardening an easier task is the lightness and looseness of the soil. River bottoms are so to begin with and this condition has been improved through the use of humus, manure and wood ashes, by working green cover crops into the soil and by the avoidance of chemicals injurious to soil bacteria. Even so the garden will be a nip and tuck contest all through the long summer. The sprouting of weed seeds broadcast lavishly by each flood is terrifying to see. New weeds keep appearing, more troublesome than the old. Dry weather will come, perhaps as early as April; or April

104

may be so cold and wet that the seeds do not come up. Raccoons and squirrels may invade the corn; nothing is safe from rabbits. Turtles devour tomatoes and melons. The dogs usually keep groundhogs at a distance but countless birds find choice food in the garden, sunflowers and corn in particular. Moles have a field day in the soft ground, and mice are always with us.

Yet the seeds and plants will come through if given half a chance. Unfavorable weather does not last, the varmints never eat everything and the outcome is never as bad as it might be. In the best years some crops will fail and a poor growing season is often marked by some brilliant and unexpected success. We have learned to make do with what is available, eating the same vegetable day after day with relish. A little imagination in its preparation or combination gives a pleasing variety. Ever try gooseberries and rhubarb together, or peanuts in cooked tomatoes?

We take our gardening seriously for it is the keystone of our living here. Most of our food comes from it, and rich rewards to the spirit as well. Only a gardener can realize the satisfaction of living close to the earth, in harmony with the system of nature, of knowing how to direct the forces which cover the earth with verdure so that his cherished plot of ground will produce harvests that nourish and delight him. It is no punishment to get your living by the sweat of your brow.

Every crop has some particular virtue. Some come early, some stand a frost, some are easy to raise, some are especially nutritious or have a rare flavor. One of our favorite vegetables is okra. It is a sturdy hot-weather plant that never fails, worth growing just for its large, pale-yellow flowers. Its one fault is overproduction. Since experiments with canning and drying have not solved the problem of what to do with the surplus, we eat large quantities of it, often three days running. Those who say they do not like okra should taste some that Anna has cooked—cut in small cylinders, fried in butter and eaten without delay.

A main crop is soybeans, not the field variety but large ones which are green even when dry. They may be cooked as lima beans are, fresh or dried, and they are the only soybeans which are tender. Soybean plants and beans are the rabbit's favorite garden crop. I plant a few here and there in the garden just for him, and he will seek them out, leaving other beans untouched. To protect the soybeans we want for ourselves, I surround them with a low fence of chicken wire. This, though effective against rabbits, did not keep out a groundhog, who had wandered into the garden regardless of the dogs. When he came to the bean fence, he burrowed under it, surfacing in the midst of the soybeans. What luck, he thought, plenty of choice food and a fence to keep the dogs out.

For each crop there seems to be a wild creature intent on devouring it. Birds work on the sunflowers, moles and mice on the peanuts underground, rabbits on the leaves. The birds begin as soon as the sunflower seeds are formed. Chickadees, titmice, cardinals and downy woodpeckers

106

are the chief raiders. They soon strip the earliest heads, which are volunteers from seed scattered with the compost, and often of immense size. Later the birds seem less voracious but seldom does a sunflower head mature with no seeds missing. I inspect the plants, now much taller than I, every two or three days, and cut down the heads the birds have started on. To get the seeds off the heads I use a bit of flat stick that has a few small nails driven through it near the end, like the teeth of a rake. The seeds are dried in the sun on a screen protected by another screen. During the winter I remove the kernels by cracking open the seeds in a hand grist mill and putting them handfuls at a time into a pail of water. The kernels sink, the empty hulls are skimmed off. The birds are eager to pick over the hulls, finding every bit of kernel. The whole seeds are shared with the birds in snowy weather. By that time we have forgiven their summer robbery.

The goats have a share in other garden crops. Sometimes we plant grain sorghum, which like corn furnishes both grain and forage. Since the goats insist on leafy hay, some alfalfa and soy hay is produced for them, and it is also made from leafy vegetables—chard, comfrey, parsnip and beet tops, bean and pea vines. They eat a large part of the squash harvest. In the latter part of winter I get root vegetables out of the storage pit for them, mostly beets, turnips and parsnips; or there may be huge mangelwurzels grown just for them.

Each product of the garden is handled many times

before it reaches winter storage. Over and over we admire
the singular beauty of form, color, texture or design that
each has. Consider a heap of squashes in the September
sun, the contrast between brown butternut and the great
cushaw with its bizarre striping of dark green on its
curved ivory body. Sunflower seeds on their cushion lie in
a pattern of interlacing circles, all in sober tones of gray
that seem to repent the wanton flowering of summer.
Jade green soybeans in bristly, dark-brown pods and rich
yellow corn in faded husks. It is a near miracle to pull
tapering orange carrots out of the ground or dark-red
beets; sweet potatoes most of all, so varied in shape and
size, of such a golden color.

The slanting sun is warm, the sky above the tawny
earth is of deepest blue. The gardener harvests much
that was never planted.

A delightful by-product of the garden, one that we are
in a position to enjoy fully, is a plunge into the river after
a stint of work in the burning sun. Beginning with the
first days hot enough to raise a sweat, and regardless of
muddy water, it becomes so much a part of the garden
ritual that Anna calls me to dinner early enough to allow
time for it.

Although the days may not be as hot and sticky as in
July, I enjoy going into the river most in the quiet and
sunny weather of the fall. The river, then at its clearest,
is of an intense blue which contrasts with the pale
golden-green shores. The shallow water at our landing is

warm, the muddy bottom of early summer has become firm sand. Even more than other pleasures of late summer, this one is enhanced by the thought that the fine, warm days are numbered.

I have found no one who sympathizes with my insistence on gardening by hand, without the use of any machine. So many times have the advantages of a garden tractor or tiller been pointed out to me that I half believe the argument myself and am apologetic and evasive in my replies. That is my weakness. My strength returns when I am alone in the garden, working with some beloved tool, the birds whistling overhead. Even on a sultry July morning, when not a breath of air stirs, when the sun's heat is magnified by the encircling trees, and weeds are sprouting everywhere, not even then could I welcome one of those nondescript, unlovable gadgets, brightly painted and streamlined, which make an intolerable noise and smell bad. They get the work done, you say? I say they are expensive and insidiously destructive. I will get the work done in my own way. Save time? The best use of time is to enjoy it, as I do when working in peaceful silence. I am surprised that anyone with a love for growing things will take up with artificial contrivances that come between him and nature, which break the spell woven by all the delicate garden influences, the songs of birds and insects, the sound of rustling leaves, the smell of freshly turned soil, the direct contact with the earth. What is he in the garden for?

Along in October, when a killing frost has put an end to the growth of summer, except for the hardy greenery of turnips, kale and the like, you decide that the goats may as well come into the garden to nibble on the cover crop of young wheat, the remaining cornstalks and bean vines. Garden work is about done for this year and the time has come to think seriously about firewood. One last planting remains to be made and that is the cold frame, upon which we depend for salad greens in winter. Of course there will be celery and Chinese cabbage, transplanted to boxes in the cellar, but leafy greens must come from the frame. In it we plant, when the autumn's dryness has passed, leaf lettuce, loose-head lettuce, spinach, kale, a loose-leaf celery cabbage, lamb's-lettuce, and parsley. Protected by the glass or plastic cover (we used plastic until a thoughtful friend gave us some salvaged storm sash with glass in them), plants will grow until severe cold sets in. Even then they will not freeze if given some extra covering on the coldest nights. The secret is to have the cover of the cold frame even with the ground, and the planting surface well below it. What a joy it is, in the bleakness of winter, to raise the cover and see the tender plants within, as fresh and green as in May. Late in the winter when the sun is warmer, they all start to grow afresh and continue to supply our salad bowl until the spring greens come in.

The fine October weather was broken at last by a rainy spell of several days, dark, mild and drizzling. A wind arose, southwest at first, then from the west, the clouds breaking up. Now it blows hard from the northwest, raising whitecaps which break against the bar. There is never any doubt about such a wind. It will continue until the sky is swept clear and in the calm, starry night frost will strike.

Our first thought is for the garden. We once more pick over the tomatoes, okra and green beans. I bring in the last hamper of sweet peppers, green and bright red as if enameled. More celery is dug up and carried into the cellar, the rest can be protected with a tarpaulin. Lettuce and Chinese cabbage will survive some frost. We will see how cold the evening becomes.

I go down to the windy river shore, check on the johnboat, turn loose the minnows. Too rough to bait up this evening. This might be the end of fishing for this season. Some green stuff in the garden is worth gathering up for the goats and nothing more can be done.

The wind lessens toward sundown but is reluctant to give up entirely. With twilight the cold increases. Cold; you could not imagine how it was, during the heat of summer, and it was thought of with some dread on the first chilly mornings of autumn. But now it is here, my spirits rise. Summer could offer no sunset like this one. Exciting new vistas have been opened by the wind and dry leaves are rustling everywhere. How beautiful is a bare tree, a symbol of the tautness and simplicity of winter!

I gather up an armload of firewood to take into the house, my thoughts on the cozy fireside; but I linger in the cold, watching the fading afterglow and its reflection where the river is smooth. Have we nothing new to undertake? It was in October that we went down to the river to build the shantyboat, in another October that we began to build this house in Payne Hollow. It is the time for adventure. The year should begin with the first frost.

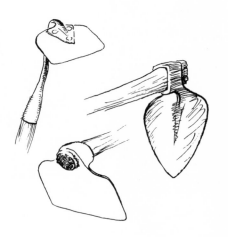

At whatever hour we returned from a trip to town, the two brown dogs were eagerly waiting for us on the dock. Black and white Tray, a very busy dog, dashed out at the last moment.

13

Underneath our house is an old-fashioned country cellar, dirt-floored and stone-walled, with dusty timbers close overhead, lighted only by the door through which you enter. According to suburban standards it might seem merely a damp hole-in-the-ground, yet it is a basic part of our establishment. It keeps food cool in summer, protects it from freezing in winter. Moreover, our cellar has a deep significance. We feel more secure with our house firmly rooted in the earth, and the provender stored there is of more value than a pocketful of money.

I like the cellar because it is so honest. It makes no effort to impress anyone and its dust is there for everyone to see who cares to enter.

The cellar is most inviting now in late fall when the garnered harvest makes it a miniature county fair. The wide shelves are loaded with neat rows of full jars, a colorful parade which celebrates the ripening of summer. It was back in April that we gathered the poke in those jars. Next are ranks of spinach and green peas. Farther along are blackberries, tawny gooseberries, golden honey, platoons of redcoat tomatoes, green beans whose uncut pods stand on end—for Anna takes pride in the appearance of her canning. Pale jars of catfish march next to a sanguine block which is goat meat, canned in winter.

Under the shelves are boxes with screens on top to keep mice from nibbling the potatoes which are inside. The cellar is walled on only three sides, the fourth being a sloping earth bank where the squash are laid. Around the edges of the floor are boxes and old buckets containing growing celery and Chinese cabbage whose greenness gives the effect of a conservatory, which is what the cellar really is.

Surely no two people could eat all this accumulation of food in one winter, even with the help of guest, dogs and goats. Why store up more than we need? I have an idea that squirrels and mice pack away all the seeds and nuts they can lay their paws on. The winter is long, and who knows, the harvest might be scanty next year. Anna will let nothing go to waste, but sometimes asks why I plant so much. I reply that it is a rule of nature to be lavish with seeds; yet I have learned to be moderate and my aim is to have small plantings coming on at well-timed intervals.

Not all of our food comes from the garden. The goats produce milk and meat, a stand of bees gives us some honey. We take fish from the river, catfish mostly, by trotline in spring, summer and fall. Until river minnows became scarce, the baiting of the line in the evening was as much a part of the day as the sunset. We all rowed out together in the johnboat, and Anna sat in the stern with the dogs close to her, while I baited from the bow. The memory of innumerable summer evenings on the river under a mellow sky fading toward night will stay with us

116

always. In winter, when conditions are right, schools of small shad leave the muddy river to enjoy the clear water of the creek. A bucketful, or a tubful can be dipped up easily and they are delicious, grilled over hot coals. Fish are a smaller part of our diet nowadays. Perhaps they are harder to catch, or I have become lax in my attempts.

Like good shantyboaters we keep an eye open for whatever is in season on the hills and in the woods. Of course we refrain from picking up anything the owner of the land might want for himself. A drifting shantyboater need not be so scrupulous. It is only a more permanent resident, however, who can attain a true understanding of the countryside and of his neighbors.

The town stores contribute little in the way of food. We skim through the supermarket in wonder and amazement, but come out with only such commonplace items as paper towels, matches, salt, canning supplies and yeast. Sometimes we take a flyer in lemons, oranges, raisins or liver. Nothing we really need is perishable, so a year's supply could be kept on hand. For that matter, we could do without all of it and be independent of town stores.

Hardware, goat feed, clothes and library books are more nearly indispensable. While in town for them, we may as well stop in our favorite grocery store. It relaxes the tension of being in town, for the smiling proprietor is a good friend. He may have some bargain bananas and bones for the dogs.

If forced to live in town we would get more of our

provisions from the mill which supplies the farmers with stock feed. Cattle are fed more sensibly than humans, and at much less cost. As it is, we get blackstrap from the feed store, and as long as it was possible, wheat germ.

There is a spirit of adventure in the air when we determine to take a trip to town. Lists are written, the mail, empty sacks and the like made ready, a lunch packed. The dogs droop with disappointment and Tray looks at us reproachfully; they do not attend us to the riverbank. We row across—that is always an adventure and never the same—and feel that one stage is accomplished when we find that the car is still there, with no flat tires. It starts, second stage. The narrow road along the river around Plowhandle Point is never monotonous. After ten miles we enter town hopefully. Soon after lunch, which of course we eat along the waterfront, the tide turns. We accomplish the most necessary errands and beat a retreat as quickly as possible. We are home again when we reach the riverbank and see our johnboat waiting for us.

Yet through the years a liking for the town has grown within us, fostered partly by the old buildings and streets, partly by the merchants. How friendly and considerate they are, and how patiently they get all that stock together and wait for us to come for what we need.

The pleasure of seeing
mother and kids together
is one of the intangible rewards
of keeping goats...
Life for the kids is an unmixed joy.
They eat and sleep with abandon.
Their frisking play would bring a
smile to the soberest countenance.

14

Sometimes the question is asked, in a tone that implies remissness on our part, "Why don't you keep chickens?" Practical and economic reasons could be brought forward in answer, but the fact that neither of us would be made happier by having a flock of the flighty birds on the place is enough. This seems unfair to chickens when I think how picturesque a flock of them used to be, contentedly scratching in a farm barnyard. It is a sight rarely seen nowadays, however, when chickens and eggs are big business. Likewise, few farmers around here keep a cow for their own use. They buy milk from a "dairy" in the city which makes deliveries on all the country roads. The practice of keeping goats for milk is thoroughly scorned; yet it had long appealed to me. Although I had rarely seen them, goats seemed to be individuals, with more personality than cows. I admired their independence. They were a sort of shantyboat animal, able to maintain themselves on fringe land.

At first Anna took little interest in my proposal to get some goats, being satisfied with our present source of milk, which was to buy the canned or powdered kind from the store; but as I rehearsed the advantages of fresh goat milk, and other benefits as well, such as meat, and manure for the garden, she began to look upon the idea more favorably. At length we determined to proceed, and as soon as our establishment in Payne Hollow was fairly complete, took the first steps.

We began by reading the available books on the subject. Much of their advice was too complicated for us, but we did follow it in one particular, and built a stable for the goats before getting them. It was located at the upstream end of the higher garden where it merges into the woods, a convenient place for all concerned and not too near the house. A little digging had to be done, some rough stonework laid up on the lower side, a few johnboat loads of boards ferried across and carried up to the building site, luckily not far from the river. It is a pleasant, shady spot, and the rough building, framed with poles cut nearby and driftwood timbers, in size about ten by fourteen feet with a loft, would make a good cabin for people to live in. A small yard was fenced adjacent to the stable and then we began to look for two suitable she-goats in earnest.

They were not easy to find in this country where a herd of goats means "brush goats," a bunch of nondescripts kept for land-clearing purposes. After considerable scouting about the spring countryside, we thought ourselves fortunate to acquire a pair of mature does of Toggenburg breeding, each with a good-sized kid, all for ten dollars. We hauled them to the river in our trailer, the chassis of our old camping trailer, for which I had made slat sides. We were a little uneasy about ferrying them across in the johnboat, but the water disturbed them not at all, nor did their new quarters. We were the ones who had to make an adjustment, and it soon became evident that there was more to learn than we had bargained for. The keeping of animals is a strict discipline and it should not be undertaken lightly. You must give at least as much as you get and accept the hard truth that you are servant, not master.

In the summer the does made it plain to us that a herd was not complete without a buck. Goofus made everybody happy. He was all white, shaggy, a noble animal; yet he struck us at first sight as a rather comical figure, with a long, Santa Claus beard.

Our flock increased rapidly and before long numbered fourteen. They looked like fifty, straggling through the woods or along the shore, and we were proud of them. Fourteen was too many, however; too many to feed, too many for the little stable in winter, and they produced more milk and meat than our small household could consume. We canned meat for use in warm weather and I smoked sausage and a sort of jerked meat in the fish smoker. Anna turned out large quantities of cottage cheese and yogurt, and also undertook the making of hard cheese. A long and detailed procedure, it called for some special equipment, such as a cheese press, which we contrived from a gallon can and some sticks of wood, the pressure being supplied by a piece of railroad iron and several bricks as required. The cheeses were excellent in flavor and texture, though not always the same because of variations in temperature beyond our control. These measures enabled us to use all the milk, but we still must exercise unrelenting control over the herd to keep it within bounds.

The books on goat keeping recommend the separation of the kids from their mothers at birth; a cruel act, but we tried it. This involved teaching the kids to drink and feeding them out of a pan or nursing bottle. When they were very young we had to get up at least twice during the night, put on outdoor clothes, build a fire to heat milk, go down to the stable in the wintry darkness and fumble about with the uncooperative little ones. Although several advantages were claimed for this plan, its defects were obvious. We put the book aside and let nature do it her way. No benefits derived from their separation could be worth more than the pleasure of seeing mothers and kids together. That is one of the intangible rewards of keeping goats.

Several bucks have followed Goofus, for it seems best not to keep the same one too long—Newt, Booster, Sassafras (a fraternity mascot in his very young days), Samson, Prince Igor. It is hard to remember each one, to us they are all the same animal; all of them gentle, reasonable, less intelligent but more amiable than the reserved does. The dignified old fellows with their long horns present an awesome appearance to strangers, but they would hurt no one intentionally.

The buck, according to the books, should be kept from the rest of the herd. We tried this with Newt. I made a pen and shelter in the shade by the creek, fenced it in and put Newt there with a youngster for company. He would not stay. Again and again I strengthened the fence, but Newt could get through or over and we would see him trotting off eagerly in the direction of his does. At length I succeeded in making a fence that would hold him. He bawled without ceasing and refused to eat—until we turned him loose.

There is no serious drawback to letting buck and does live together, except that the date of breeding cannot always be known. The buck is certainly more contented and better natured, your herd is complete and the does are happier, too. So much for the books; yet they do contain valuable information and we consult them frequently.

When the kids are well started and strong I put them in the "kid pen" at night. This is a large stall with a big window and private yard. The kids have hay and grain to eat, but of course are at first unhappy to be separated from their mothers. They let out continuing bleats, bawls and squeaks until darkness comes and they go to sleep. At break of dawn I milk the does, then leave the kids with them for the rest of the day. Thus we get our share of the milk, the kids have plenty and they are no trouble.

The first summer we tried staking the goats out to browse, but this was so thoroughly objectionable to them and to us that I fenced in some of our woods around the stable for a pasture. In a short time the goats had eaten every leaf and twig they could reach. The only solution was to turn them loose in the woods which surround us.

Seldom does the herd fail to come home in the evening,

sometimes early in the afternoon. For us the faint tinkling of the leader's bell announces that the end of the day is near and that all is well. We often watch them file along the path and suddenly rush down the last slope, even the old buck kicking up his heels.

Unless rain is falling the goats start off eagerly in the dewy morning, enter the pathless woods, nibble here and there, go down to the river or creek for a drink, always on the move except for their long siestas. If a shower comes up they shelter under the cave-like overhang of the cliffs at the top of the hill, where they doze by the hour, unconscious of hunger, thirst or time. Whatever they do, it is as a group, and any one of them becomes panicky if separated from the rest. This free ranging is a goat's idea of happiness. It lightens our responsibility because no other pasturage is necessary, no hay in summer, not much in winter. They can always find something to eat in the woods, if nothing more than dry leaves, twigs, bark and juniper needles.

Goats suit our needs and capacities better than cows, who would not fare so well in the grassless woods. A cow gives too much milk, they eat too much, and butchering one is a formidable undertaking for one person.

When I was faced with my first butchering of a goat, I reflected that I had killed and cleaned many groundhogs, or woodchucks, if you prefer. Reasoning that a goat would be like a larger groundhog I went about butchering it in the same manner. The operation turned out well. More practice improved my method and gear until now I

126

can perform the job quickly and painlessly. It is rigorous work, early in the coldest morning. The decision is the hardest part: which one, and when? There is usually something against each possible choice and time, and you are only too willing to postpone the sacrifice until the signs are more favorable. It is best to go ahead, and once begun, all is easy; the routine carries through. As to those people who ask, "How can you butcher anything, most of all one of your own goats?", I say: I would knock a goat in the head rather than mistreat it, or condemn it to a solitary life, underfeed it, let it live to be old and infirm, or tie it to a stake all day. Our goats live a happy life until the blow falls and it is suddenly over. No regrets, no mourning. The rest of the herd never hold it against me, they come in that evening as if nothing had happened.

Should not all who eat meat be willing to do their own butchering? If the eating of meat has so much against it, perhaps it should be given over entirely.

We cannot say how much it costs us to produce a quart of milk. More, probably, than we think it does; yet we are sure that store milk would be more expensive. Certainly it would not be as good as goat milk, fresh and untampered with, nor could we buy the abundance we now enjoy. Of course, we could get along on store milk, and on a smaller quantity than we now have. Quality and plenty, how much are they worth in cash? Such values cannot be reduced to figures, and that is one reason, the main one, why we do not keep books. There are intangible losses, too—in time, worry and tribulation. No item is purely profit or loss. On a winter evening I might prefer to remain by the fireside, but the goats must be fed and milked. Once in the stable, I enjoy its particular kind of warmth and coziness, and the lantern casts its spell. The stable is a world of its own, antithetical to the house world. How often have I sat on a three-legged milking stool among the munching goats, looking out of the window at the rough hillside when larkspur is blooming or snow is drifted over the roots and rocks. If the goats do not come home at evening I am provoked with them and would rather do something else than climb the hill to get the inconsiderate beasts; yet my mood improves as I climb the well-known trail. First I look along the base of the cliff, where they are most likely to be. The sun is behind me, low on the western horizon. Its level rays strike the bulging rock face above me and it glows in the golden light. Up there, on ledges and in niches, stand the goats, motionless as if carved from the stone. They look down on me with steady, unrevealing gaze; yet they are no doubt amused at my clumsy scrambling.

The round of the goats' year is never quite the same, but often in late autumn, when they are producing little or no milk, and are consequently not so hungry, the stable loses its attraction for them. Led by a wise old doe, they yield to wanderlust and explore farther into the woods, feeding on fresh fallen leaves and ripening seeds. The stable is lonely and deserted. I search their old haunts

128

about the cliffs, straining to hear the delicate sound of their bell, to which so many wood sounds are similar that I am often given false hopes. I might pass close and not see the herd, standing motionless, their brown coloring fading into the autumn hues. After two or three nights out they all return to the fold, unconcerned as ever, though wary about entering the stable, as if wolves might have taken over in their absence.

Colder weather and increased appetite, due in part to the growing kids they carry, keep them coming in and the winter routine is established. I begin to feed them hay as well as grain, and their share of garden harvest, squash first, later the roots which were buried in the ground on top of the late potatoes. To the garden hay has been added that made by cutting and curing stinging nettles, also other weeds the goats like, and forest leaves, of which many sacks are filled in the autumn. Some of their grain is ear corn, which we glean in the extensive bottom across the river after the mechanical corn picker has done its work. It is a pleasant way to spend a golden afternoon in October, walking up and down the long rows, a sack over one's shoulder, pausing to look up at the novel views of home hills and river. This gleaning is becoming unprofitable due to improvements in the pickers, which rarely miss an ear.

When I contemplate the amount of grain consumed by the goats I wonder if we could not save much labor and trouble by eating the grain ourselves and ceasing to support the hungry animals.

Early winter is the time for the new kids to arrive. For this event the does prefer solitude, and they will often go off into the brush alone, hunting for a secluded spot. I have made long searches for an expectant mother who did not come in with the herd, keeping my ears open as well as my eyes, for the shrill peeping of the newly born has often guided me to the spot. It is easier for all of us when the births occur in the stable. This avoids possible losses and worry. Anna and I do the worrying, not the does, and we are definitely more excited. What a hopeless creature is a newborn kid, wet, cold and weak, lying in a pool of slime. The mother confidently sets to licking it, or the twins or triplets, dry. It struggles to its feet and is promptly knocked over by the mother's continued licking. At last it stands on shaky legs, and by instinct searches for the food which will sustain its life, poking its little muzzle in the empty air until it contacts its mother, usually at the wrong end. At this point the goatherd can sometimes be of assistance, for the little one, perhaps the third of a set of triplets, may be too weak to manage alone. It is miraculous, the strength the kid derives almost instantly from the mother's rich milk. Soon he is warm and dry, and able to shake himself, though still wobbly. Next day he is usually strong and lively and he makes a pass at playing with his brother or sister. Their doubtful beginning is forgotten, life becomes an unmixed joy. They eat and sleep with abandon, and their frisking play would bring a smile to the soberest countenance.

The goats would get along, perhaps be happier, without our care and provision. They could fend for themselves, given range enough. Indeed, Peck Hill may some day harbor a flock of wild goats who shelter under the cliff, drink from the spring and roam untended fields long after the race of men has passed away.

There is a fascination about the distant tones of a bell sounding across the water—

Who is there?

15

Soon after our settling in Payne Hollow we noticed a small shantyboat drifting on the slow current, close to the far shore. Instead of continuing on down the river, it tied up at Lee's Landing. We expected it to move on downstream after a short stay, but when the river fell there it was, resting comfortably on the bank under the cottonwoods, a weatherbeaten craft, not much larger than our shantyboat had been. It fit into the river landscape as naturally as an old snag and soon became part of the river shore, a point on which the eye could rest as it surveyed the sweep of river.

On our next trip across we met the lone occupant. He was Bill Shadrick, the last survivor of the race of shantyboaters in these parts. His birthplace was a boat moored at the time a short distance above Payne's Landing and most of his life was passed on this stretch of river; a favorite station of his was at Big Six, on the Indiana side under Plowhandle Point. Becoming lonely there after the death of an old crony, he had moved down to Lee's Landing to be near the O'Neal boys, who were farmers and fishermen.

Although Bill was a good neighbor he did not come across to Payne Hollow often enough to disturb its solitude; yet we liked having him close by, and it was comforting to see his dim light, the more so on a rough winter night, for it reminded us that the black void was inhabited, if thinly, by friends.

On the shantyboat we had been loners, avoiding towns and settlements, making friends where we chanced to meet them and moving on to remote places. Now that our home was fixed and immovable we hoped that a suitable balance between solitude and society—an abundance of solitude and not too much society—would be our lot.

Our first callers were neighbors from up on the ridge who had become acquainted with us when our shantyboat lay over at Payne Hollow. It was pleasant to sit with them on a quiet Sunday afternoon, talking and looking down on the river. The long lives of some of them reached back to a past which has just about disappeared. They would tell us how Payne Hollow used to be when steamboats were running, how they drove cattle down to the landing or loaded a barge with locust posts. The unhurried rhythm of their speech sometimes rose to poetry.

The old-timers are children of the soil. As each one passes away, an empty space is left which will not be filled by the rising generation, formed under urban influences.

As the word was spread through the country that something a little out of the ordinary was to be seen down in Payne Hollow, and that visitors were welcome,

134

more and more people came to see us. Many of them were strangers, but they knew or were related to a friend of ours—the whole county seems to be one family—and we got along very well. The rough trail and steep climb never deterred the country people, not even the old and infirm. Almost every Saturday and Sunday afternoon someone came straggling down the hill, often a group or family; or boys and girls, happy to have a new place to go. The small fry swam in the river, skipped rocks from the bar and picked up mussel shells, relics of the days when "shellers" lived at Payne's Landing. To many of them the river was a new experience and a surprising number had never been out in a small boat. Maintaining a conversation with the young people was hard work as they were so often nearly mute; but we persevered, Anna the most, with some encouraging results.

After the Sunday callers had gone, we read the names which had just been written in our swelling guest book and found we had already forgotten the persons to whom they belonged; or we had never learned, as formal introductions are not considered necessary in a country where everyone is already well acquainted. Yet, whenever any of them met us later in town, they expected to be recognized and their names remembered.

The Ohio River forms a more effective barrier than would be supposed. A family living on one shore may know only by hearsay who lives in a house standing in plain view across the river. Perhaps we only imagine that different traits and characteristics are to be found on the opposing sides, but there are definite though slight variations in temperature, soil and vegetation. For instance, dogwood is common across the river but rare on this side.

Living so close to the river and having a boat we often crossed to the other shore and came to know many of the people living there. If any of them wished to visit us they naturally came down to Lee's Landing and shouted for us to come over. I soon hung a sheet of iron on a tree at the landing, to be beaten as a signal to us. The sound of this gong became fixed in our subconscious mind, for we heard it quite often. Even some visitors from our side of the river found it a more convenient, and certainly an easier way, unless they were afraid of water, to get to Payne Hollow.

For anyone to whom this was strange territory, after a rough drive to that lonely shore, not sure it was the right place, and no habitation to be seen across the wide river, it was consoling to find this crude gong, and they beat it lustily with stick or stone, for the implement left there for that purpose had a way of disappearing. After a time the sheet of iron was replaced by an ordinary farm bell, which is plainly heard under favorable conditions.

There is a fascination about the distant tones of the bell sounding across the water. Who is there, with what news? Is it a dear friend long unseen, or a stranger whose coming will change the course of our lives? If the bell rings just at the moment when we are about to undertake some urgent work, or enjoy a pleasant diversion looked

136

forward to all day, it is the voice of a spiteful and perverse fate.

For several years I rowed the heavy johnboat back and forth (and Anna has done so more than once when I was absent) making the round trips for each party, a distance of two miles rowing. No wonder their conscience bothered some of our guests. They offered to row, the rare ones who were able to do so, but seldom could they handle the oars as well as I do, and for me to sit watching their ineptitude was really hard work. I honestly like to row and do not regard it as strenuous toil; but when by some riverbank deal a small, much-used outboard motor was left with us, we gave it a trial. It not only smoothed the feelings of passengers but proved to be of service on all trips when the combination of current and downstream wind would have carried the oarsman far below his landing place. Also, it made possible the carrying of long pieces of lumber or firewood, since no space had to be left open amidships for rowing.

Our objections to an outboard motor are more subtle, and not generally understood by the practical-minded. It makes a different craft out of the johnboat, a driven thing, quivering as if in pain. A motor is odorous and noisy. Even a small one spoils to some extent communion with the river. It interferes with your contemplation of sky and water and the distant view. Its noise discourages conversation, but this in some cases may be a desirable feature.

A motor gives its operator a sense of power which is

false, for anyone can run the thing. It sets you over to the far shore so quickly and easily that you have not the oarsman's pride of accomplishment; and rowing is an art that can be studied and practiced until a high degree of efficiency, coordination and rhythm is developed. Good rowing is beautiful to watch.

By its undeniable need for gasoline, a motor is another strand tying you to the city; but the greatest price I pay is agony of spirit at its erratic behavior, its failure to start or run properly. After a spell of ineffective pulling on the starting cord I feel degraded by what seems a servile relation to it.

At the present time I have gone back to rowing, and thus regained my independence. A second pair of oars is carried in case one of the passengers wants to try his hands with them—and a surprising number do.

Judging by its prevalence, the outboard motor has been accepted by the rest of the world without reluctance; not only outboards, but inboards, motorized rafts, cruisers and fancy cabin boats called houseboats. In their wake camps, cabins and trailers have sprouted along the shores, and boat harbors at close intervals. The Ohio is no longer the forsaken stream of the past, and the change is regretted by those who loved its forsakenness.

The stretch of river above and below Payne Hollow is only a little spoiled by the new order, although many pleasure boats go by on summer weekends. Now and then one stops to pay us a call and some warm friendships are nourished by these brief and widely spaced meetings.

When a strange craft pulls in to our landing we cannot guess what sort of people it is bringing. Some very nice ones come in the largest and most expensive boats. The situation is sometimes a little like that of explorers from the civilized world visiting the natives, and both parties are entertained and instructed.

A few miles upriver, perched on the most distant bluff, is a college whose buildings and lights can be faintly seen from Payne's Landing. Our contacts there have been a bonus of a sort never thought of when we came to live in such a rural place as Payne Hollow. We have made good friends, the library has been the source of our reading for these many years, and we have heard excellent music there. Wandering students often find the way to Payne Hollow, afoot or by bicycle to Lee's Landing, or down the river in a borrowed canoe. Most come the land way, in all seasons and weather. They bring with them the zest and friendliness of youth and its wild visions.

In these later days a new note is to be heard among the students who visit us. Many of them are scornful of the existing order and determined to pull out of it. Having heard that a couple are living in Payne Hollow on their own, experimenting with a self-sufficient and independent life such as they desire for themselves, they come to see how we are making out. Some are enthusiastic and interested enough to ask many questions. Others, the more radical in their views, seem disappointed, even hostile. We wonder about this attitude. It is not caused by lack of sympathy on our part. Perhaps our unspectacular way seems too much of a compromise to these zealots, who would fashion for themselves a rough life with more of the bark left on. Contentment, tolerance, order, some degree of comfort and neatness—such notions belong to the establishment.

An infrequent river voyager lands here on his way down the river, in a canoe or raft, but no more drifting shantyboats tie up at Payne's Landing as they used to do not long ago; nor do we see in these days a genuine houseboat, by which we mean a barge-like floating home, larger than a shantyboat and perhaps more respectable, shoved along by a motor boat, or even by a small sternwheeler. All true river travelers are most welcome. We like to hear even the mention of a place along the river which was once well known to us, and it is an honor to supply fresh water, milk or vegetables.

The mailbox on the road at the top of the hill is another contact with the outside world. Through it we may be informed of an impending visit, although the writer of the letter often arrives before his message, since it is my custom to pick up mail only once a week. Other letters come from members of our family and distant friends who would come in person if that were possible. Once in a while a letter contains news of just such a visit.

If it were not for the mail, I would rarely go up the hill, nor would the dogs make the run just for the trip; but they are wild with joy at the sight of the mail pouch, a small, flat bag like the one I used to carry school books

140

in. Though more sedate than the dogs, I set out each time as on an adventure, whatever the season and weather. I do not remember ever being in a hurry. After a final wave to Anna, I let my feet pick their way along the narrow path and across the footbridge. By the time the ascent is begun all trivial details, all thoughts of work and planning, have been left behind. My thoughts wander far away as I mount the stony trail. The rock ledges at the top and the belt of cedars are mountain country, and beyond I enter open fields and have distant views.

The mailbox holds forth engaging possibilities, but the mail for the most part is a lot of worldly trash, of a sort to deflate my elevated mood. After stuffing all of it in my bag I may have a few words with the folks whose mailbox is next to ours, or with some rarely seen neighbor who happens to pass by. The roadside dogs exchange greetings with our own, and then we return. The descent is less poetic and my thoughts reach home ahead of me.

Whoever comes to see us, college professor or riverbank camper, we try to let them have what they came for. A rare few want to play music with us, and for this we put everything aside. Some visitors are curious about our reasons for choosing to live away from the beaten track. Most, however, want to see our house, and in this Anna always obliges with a grace and unfailing cordiality that I never cease to admire. It is always an act of hospitality, spontaneous and sincere, and cleverly slanted to the age and sophistication of her audience. She is at her best with little girls and boys. The close attention shown by everyone is remarkable.

The fact that nearly everything in the house serves more than one purpose makes it intricate and complex, and a casual visitor is not aware of this until Anna points out the details. The wood-burning range, a unit with the fireplace, is often missed entirely. Its top is made from two junked stoves. Anna explains the drafts and how the wall oven above is heated. She pulls out the woodbox, which rolls easily on skate wheels. When the cupboard door is raised and hooked up to a string hanging from the ceiling, the astonishing array of jars and bottles on the shelves always brings out some questions. Anna opens some of the jars to show the breakfast cereal of wheat and soybeans coarsely ground, also the fragrant meal made from toasted soybeans and the soy flour used in bread. The jars for wheat flour and corn meal are empty, as I grind these fresh when needed. There are sunflower seeds to sample, black walnuts, home-grown peanuts and "peanut butter" made of the toasted soy meal moistened with vegetable oil. On one shelf is a row of herb bottles (Anna's favorites are sweet basil and summer savory) and some dried leaves and bark that go into tea— sassafras, pennyroyal, comfrey, spice bush, stinging nettle, parsley.

Other cupboards are opened—they are always ready for inspection—to reveal prosaic housekeeping equipment or some pieces of glass and china which came from

Anna's Dutch ancestors. When the bed is slid out from the corner, it never fails to create a surprise and someone is likely to remark, "Well, she never has to sweep under it." The piano usually gets little attention beyond some curiosity about how we got it down here. Anna is sometimes asked to play, and she readily does, usually a Chopin prelude, which all enjoy in one way or another.

We like to call attention to the pieces of driftwood which have been put to use—some long timbers which were once part of an old navigation dam in the river, a solid chunk for a step, a hewn cedar post at the corner and next to it a narrow door which is our prize. Never touched by a tool, it shows the action of the river's current by deep grooves in its surface, except the knots, which are in relief.

There isn't much to be seen on the upper floor behind the chimney. This part of the house was built first and was our entire living space for nearly five years while the rest was brought to completion. Its low ceiling is supported by sycamore poles, and the wide cottonwood boards which form the ceiling are removed in summer to let in the light and air coming down through the open gable. The metal fireplace once used for heat and cooking has been replaced by a cupboard, but the old water bucket is still in its corner, next to a drain made accessible by a small door which also conceals the hand basin on a sliding shelf. There are more cupboards and bookshelves, another standing bed.

The company has now seen about all there is to our

house, unless they want to go up into the attic by a folding stairway, or down to the cellar through a trap door, which some of them do. A few linger to make observations on their own, or to comment on the oil lamps with shining chimneys, or to ask about the fireplace hood which was once a piece of junk of such awkward shape that it became hammered copper. The gleam of copper and brass from shelves and corners is always noticed. These pieces are not "antiques," but honest household utensils, more relics from the old country, and still used as they were generations ago.

Our visitors assume it their privilege to ask questions, often of such a private nature that they might be answered, "that concerns us only." We have learned to be cautious in replying to personal questions, however, for they are often a sign of a real interest in our solution of problems which face everyone. It is best to answer sincerely whatever may be asked. The most unpromising person has surprised us by revealing in his turn a mind and character that deserve respect, and with a little encouragement nearly everyone has something to say that is worth listening to.

If asked, "Do you take a newspaper?" or "What do you grow in your garden?" our reply can be simple and direct, unless we choose to go into the many ramifications that are inherent in the most innocent question. In some instances words fail us. "What do you do all day?" (this to Anna) or "Do you have any children?" Replying "no"

144

to the last, we fancy a gleam in the questioner's eye which says, "I thought so. You couldn't live this way if you did"; an unfair judgment, we think, but nothing can be proven on either side by words.

The questions easiest to answer are those of a practical kind. If asked about our source of water or about fishing in the river, we give detailed explanations. Housewives are often interested in our way of doing the laundry. They imagine this to be a laborious task when done by hand, since it is generally regarded as drudgery even with the help of the most elaborate equipment. We tell the whole procedure to show them that our way has redeeming features:

Our washday begins at daybreak or before, when I must decide on the chances for dry, sunny weather. A mistake in judgment is not very serious, for we always get the clothes dry eventually, come what may. The first step is to begin heating large containers of water on the breakfast fire; outside on the terrace in summery weather, inside on the fireplace in winter. A long low bench on the terrace (perhaps the visitor who asked the question is seated on it) has a second set of legs which can be unfolded to raise the bench to a convenient height for working in the tubs without bending over them. The bench holds four tubs, two of hot water for soaking, two of cold for rinsing. In spring, summer or early fall we work on the terrace, the trees overhead changing color with the advancing year. In winter we carry bench and tubs into the house and set them up between the fireplace and the big window. Every washday has enough of the unexpected to deserve an entry in the journal, but the procedure is always the same. I rub one piece after another on an old-fashioned scrub board and toss it into the first rinse. By good fortune Anna enjoys the rinsing while I prefer to rub. Both occupations leave the mind free to wander and think about whatever comes along. This is one of the joys of washday and new, influential thoughts may turn up. By the time I have worked through the whites, the water has cooled enough for soaking the colored things. Then come my blue denims, on which a stiff brush is used. Last are the door mats, hand woven from scraps of unraveled barge ropes. Finally I scrub the terrace stones by emptying the tubs and sweeping off the water with an old broom.

After Anna, with some help on the heavier pieces, has rinsed everything through two waters, she hangs it all out to dry on lines stretched between house and woodshed, giving a carnival air to the yard. If the washing has been done inside, it is festooned from the ceiling joists on the upper level where the stove dries it quickly. Thus in winter we can wash in any kind of weather, but in other seasons a sharp lookout for a sudden shower is necessary. This much is a morning's work. As the afternoon progresses, Anna takes in the things as they dry and stows them away, sweet and fresh. I end the day by reeling in the clothesline and all is cleared away until another washday comes along in two weeks.

146

A question relative to the laundry is about our source of water. For several years I carried all of it in buckets from the river, the creek and the spring beside the creek. The different kinds of water were used for different purposes, but we had no scruples about using that from the river for nearly everything but drinking, if the spring were dry. In those days we took the laundry down to the riverbank when the water was clear enough, that I might not have to carry so many bucketfuls up to the house. It recalled camping days to build a fire on the shore, and working there in the early morning was a pleasant experience. Former inhabitants of Payne Hollow claim that the spring ran all the time, but it dries up in the late summer and fall nowadays. In order to have a more dependable supply of pure water I tried to sink a well on the riverbank, but my hand drilling struck an extensive layer of rock in every attempt. The alternative now was to build a cistern to hold rain water, a tremendous labor, it seemed at the time, equal to the carrying of buckets for years to come. Sweet water to drink, pure air to breathe, naturally grown food and such delights to the soul as space, quiet, solitude and dark nights—these rewards outweigh by far the time and energy required to achieve them. It must be admitted, however, that all the advantages of life in the country are to some extent adulterated by the foul emanations and far-reaching tentacles put forth by the cities, against which there is no defense.

Some well-meant questions I dread, or perhaps it is the

147

type of person who asks them. "Who plows your garden?" I feel an accusing finger pointed at me. "No one," I reply meekly. Feeling it necessary to say more, I explain that this alluvial soil is easy to work with a hoe, and I mulch some of it, but this is unconvincing. The common rule is to avoid all hand labor, at whatever cost. As old Newt said, "A man who has wood to cut is a fool if he doesn't use a chain saw." Who would understand if I simply stated, "I like to do it my way"?

There is much concern among our more aged guests, especially on Anna's account, about our keeping warm in winter; or what we would do if both of us were taken sick at the same time. A most vital question, one never asked outright but often hinted at, concerns our financial situation. Everyone has to have some money and the source is usually apparent. Since I do not work at a paying job, and seem never to have done so, it is assumed that we have a private income or public support. This is not so. The small amount of money we need dribbles in from here and there. We are used to "littling along." For instance, the fireplace keeps us warm to a certain degree. If the weather gets cold and windy, a fire in the furnace is in order. When winter really comes, we set up a heating stove on the upper level. In extreme cold, the cookstove burns all day and we wear extra clothes. So it is with money. The house back in town is still rented, a few paintings are sold, something has been set aside for a rainy day. The secret is, spend little and you will have plenty. How much does one need to live on? As much as

148

one has, I say. The first requirement is faith—plus imagination, freedom from prejudice, habit and public opinion; simple tastes and inexpensive pleasures. We avoid discussion of such matters. Just as healthy people are not concerned about sickness and remedies, those who are truly solvent give little thought to money.

When asked this one, we have a ready answer: "What did you do before you came to live here?" "We lived for seven years on a shantyboat." If our interrogator recovers and persists, "What before that?" I am at a loss, not having done much of anything. A life given to painting is not a subject for ordinary conversation.

There is one aspect that I mention only to the rare young men who would profit by it. That is my handiness and experience with tools. When a boy I liked to make things, was encouraged to do so and taught something about handling tools. When in high school I worked for two summers as a farmhand in the days when horses supplied power and hand work was the rule. The farmers to whom I hired out were old-timers, masters with scythe, axe and hoe. One of them, a former carpenter-contractor of the old school, was able to teach me much about the care and use of his tools, and the respect, almost reverence, that was due them. Later, to earn the money that gave me freedom to go on painting, I worked for a contractor who was building cheap houses to sell. Since I was cheap labor, it was to his advantage to use me in place of higher paid men. Thus I acquired some skill in brick and stone masonry, concrete work, painting, finish carpentry. I even substituted for the plumber. Though I never became a master craftsman, nor a specialist in anything, my rough-and-ready experience with many tools and materials has been invaluable in these days of shantyboating and homesteading. The young men and women of today who are eager to live on their own—how can they come by the necessary skill with their hands, the knowledge of building and planting? Or be inspired by a love of tools and hand work in these days of prefabrication and power? They should be aware that their shortcomings cannot be remedied by overconfidence, but with a strong enough desire, and faith, patience and time they can achieve in their own fashion whatever they undertake.

We introduced ourselves in these parts as shantyboaters, then settled in Payne Hollow, the habitation in the past of some people of questionable character. I expected to assume the lowly position accorded to an occasional farm laborer but the permanent residents of the community had other ideas. They preferred to consider me as an "artist" and (most of them) to call me Mr. Hubbard. That an artist lives here is an additional attraction to Payne Hollow and visitors often ask to see some of my paintings. In most cases I would prefer to refuse, from an innate dislike to show myself in any form, but I overcome this and lead the way to my workshop. This is a comedown after the house, being nothing more than a dusty workshop—your painting shed, someone called it—and not what an

150

artist's studio is expected to be. The paintings I display usually draw a response, however, for I have learned by experiment which ones appeal and have at hand a small collection, most being of a documentary sort. Nearly everyone feels obliged to say which ones he or she likes in order of preference, and I listen to the same questions over and over—

"How long did it take you to paint this one?"

"Where was that taken from?"

"Is that steamboat the *Delta Queen*?" (It never is.)

"How much is this one?"

I observe reactions to my paintings carefully and am sometimes gratified by a preference for one which demands more of the viewer. I take more seriously the remarks of the unsophisticated than I do the learned jargon (or silence or faint praise) of the rare critic who finds his way here. Now and then a sensitive, honest person is moved by one of my paintings. If this were not so, I could have no faith in them myself.

After everyone has gone we sometimes ask ourselves why do people come here, and what do they get?

It might be expected that two people who are jointly trying to live as they want to, who are following a path uncommon to the rest of the world, would be regarded as "queer." No one does so, or at least we have not noticed it. Perhaps our innocence saves us. This is sincere. We do not feel apart from our neighbors, or different from them.

I like to think that a deeper and unrealized motive brings these strangers to Payne Hollow. It is not only the young radicals who distrust the world of today. Many people apparently conservative and orthodox harbor an underlying reaction against the artificiality and complexity of urban life (such as even country people live nowadays). A subconscious longing seldom put into words comes out in such expressions as, "These days everyone is in too much of a hurry. Wish we could get out of the rat race and have a place like yours." They do not really wish anything of the kind. This world of today is too beguiling, too comfortable, too exciting. It offers protection and acceptance. Yet the inward doubt and desire, though too feeble to be effective, are hidden in the minds of many, and perhaps they come here to see if there could really be an escape into a way that is less complex and more natural than the one to which they hopelessly resign themselves.

In these later days we are visited by strangers less often, and are likely to have even a Sunday afternoon alone. It is a precious time, and having put aside our workday thoughts and clothes, we are happy to devote the long hours to pursuits which, though they bring no practical results, give some point to our weekday activity.

Our after-dinner reading time is extended into the afternoon, and then if still not interrupted, we make some music together, essaying once again the bold themes and soaring melodies of some sonata for piano and violin for which our technical abilities are inadequate, but whose essence is revealed and deeply felt; or we may go back into the past to the simple and carefree rhythms

152

written when life must have been less clouded than it is today. Sometimes Anna tunes the cello and with my viola we play duos never composed for those instruments, perhaps an aria from a churchly cantata of passionate fervor. We play on, regardless of the bell which might be summoning us, or of the barking dogs who think they hear voices in the distance.

The declining sun and failing light will at length remind us of inexorable chores. We put away our instruments, ever thankful for this ephemeral pleasure which yet has power to transfigure existence.

As I prepare to go down to the stable or riverbank, to revive smoldering fires as the evening chill settles upon us, or to accomplish some quick strokes in the garden for which conditions are just right, I try to conceive a life of more leisure, a condition which men have ever been trying to achieve by various means—by forcing slaves or captives in war to do the menial work, or by letting it devolve upon womenfolk, or by hiring servants, and nowadays by innumerable machines and gadgets. This last solution allows everyone to play the master, but it is well known that machines are in a way to become masters of men.

From my experience with leisure I have learned that too much of it is not good. Having not quite as much as you would like gives a greater value to the time you do have, and it gives a drive and conciseness to your productions.

Anyway, I prefer to do my own work, lowly as it may

seem to the proud ones for whom the use of arms and legs is to be avoided at all costs. It is a simpler way, and the rewards are independence, and satisfaction of accomplishment, and the pleasure of being out-of-doors when the sun sets.

"The studio"

Bill Shadrick's weather beaten craft, not much larger than our shanty boat had been, resting comfortably on the bank under the cottonwood trees.

16

In our early days on the river, steamboats and
shantyboats were as much a part of it as willow trees and
sandbars. Now, twenty-five years later, a real working
steamboat is not to be found, and as for shantyboats,
there are none within our range, not even an abandoned
hulk left where it had been beached out after a flood—
except Bill Shadrick's, and it was just across the river
from us.

Bill's nearness we regarded as a fortunate circumstance.
Few works of man harmonize so well with nature as a
shantyboat, itself almost a natural creation; and Bill
would have been a friend worth having anywhere. He
was an unusual person, talking little yet saying much.
The world seemed to come to his door, and he was
amused by its foolishness. He was all the time cheerful
and friendly, yet with a dignified reserve. To chat with
him, having crossed the river on our way to town, made
the trip easier, and to find him there in the cool shade on
our return helped us to shed our town thoughts more
quickly. He became a sort of gatekeeper for us, watching
over our johnboat while we were gone, and informing us
if anyone had come to ring the bell during our absence.
He extracted a report from all our visitors, much to the
entertainment of both parties. It would have been a
reserved person indeed who would not be pleased to talk

with Bill while waiting for me to cross the river. He assured newcomers that this was the right place and instructed them in the proper procedure of bell ringing, or rang it himself, in some cases. If a person had been here before, he was remembered as an old friend, and they had much to talk about. Bill told everyone the news of Payne Hollow, to the extent that we never had any surprises for our guests—"Oh yes, Bill told me that."

When the river rose sixteen feet above pool stage, Bill's boat came afloat—unless it sank. That was sometimes an open question for the hull was old and leaked badly, even though Bill had put water in the bilge beforehand to swell the planking. Much pumping and bailing had to be done, often through the night, in which labor Bill might be assisted by some of his cronies.

To avoid having to go through this crisis so often, the old man decided to beach out on top of the bank between the fringe of trees and the cornfield, but a flood that was high enough to make this maneuver possible did not come before the boat had to be abandoned. He dismantled the cabin and built a shack of the salvaged material upon the higher level. This was heavy labor and we admired Bill for undertaking it at seventy-four years; yet when I went over one day with some tools, he would not have my assistance.

"You go home. If I let you help I will have to work harder than I want to. By myself I can set my own pace."

The little house was finished before cold weather and

all its cracks stuffed with shreds from an old mattress. It was a typical riverbank shack, as cozy a home as a man could wish for. I envied his having only that small space to heat.

During the winter that followed, the perverse river rose over the bank and half submerged the walls of Bill's new home. He made no complaint, rather treated it as a good joke on himself. Long experience had taught him how to get along with the river.

While waiting for his house to come out in the dry, Bill stayed with one of the O'Neal boys in the old Lee place, there being plenty of room in the tall, rambling farmhouse with six gables. It is still a landmark from the river, which it faces, turning its back on the present road. On the north slope of one of the barn roofs the original slate is still in place and one can make out in large, faint letters formed by a different color of slate, J. H. LEE.

Bill had set his cabin at the very edge of the bank, regardless of warnings that the river would undermine it; and this happened shortly. Bill outwitted the river this time by dying suddenly. He may have had a premonition of this event and accordingly put the least possible effort into the building of his cabin.

One spring day I had seen him planting a long row of Kentucky Wonder pole beans. "Every hill I plant, I think to myself—what am I doing this for? I'll never eat all them beans."

He never did believe in unnecessary labor, certainly not for posterity.

With the removal of an old landmark, a tree, a
building or a person, the character of the countryside
deteriorates. No amount of improvement can make up
for the loss; there is never a change for the better. The
shore opposite us, the distant valley of Lee's Creek,
the road winding down the hill make up the same lovely
view from Payne Hollow as always; but now the eye
turns quickly away from the weekenders' shiny trailers
which have replaced Bill's boat. One must accept these
changes and make the best of them. This will be the
landscape the rising generation will know, and they will
not understand what has been lost.

Will they understand the value of such a man as Bill
Shadrick? Or will his successor be classed as one of the
poor, a non-contributing member of society, which will
make an effort to improve him? Instead, he should be
cherished as a living example of a man able to go his own
way and not be overcome by the pressures to conformity.
Bill never worked hard or steadily unless it pleased him
to do so; he had no worries about the future; he was little
concerned about money or the lack of it, nor did
ownership of land bother him. Many substantial citizens,
harassed and driven in this vexatious world, might well
envy a man who possessed the leisure and disposition to
sit in the shade on a summer afternoon and be contented
to do nothing more than look over the river to the hazy,
distant hills.

It will be asked, "What if everyone should live this
way?" An idle question. There is always a plenty of

160

hands to do the world's drudgery. A real calamity would be the total disappearance of the Bill Shadricks; yet that is how it may be, some day.

Once, when Bill was beached out at Big Six, he accepted a ride into town from a friend of ours. Noting that he was a stranger, Bill asked him what had brought him to these parts. Upon learning that he had been visiting Harlan Hubbard in Payne Hollow, Bill considered a moment, then put another question: "Is he a real riverman?"

This puzzled our friend, but we can see Bill's point. He himself was indeed a real riverman, born on a shantyboat and as much a part of the river as the catfish and driftwood. On the other hand, we had come to the river by choice and to his sensitive eye some remnants of our former town environment still clung to us. He regarded us as amateurs.

Yet it could be asserted that we are closer to the river than Bill ever was. An undeniable love for the river drew us away from town and down to the shore; the boat we built there was to carry us into a new existence. This regeneration gave a direction to our lives that Anna had never before contemplated; for me it was the fulfillment of old longings; yet we were both led on by a common desire to get down to earth and to express ourselves by creating a setting for our life together which would be in harmony with the landscape.

Thus our conception of shantyboating—for we still

regard ourselves as shantyboaters even though our home is a house on shore instead of a boat—is quite different from Bill Shadrick's. It goes deeper than his, and rests on firmer ground. We live with a tautness which results in pressures and tensions from the outside world that Bill never experienced in his easygoing way. Our house, like our boat, is always in order, well arranged and clean as a pin. We cannot sit in idleness for very long at a time, letting life drift along as it will. To buy bread and coffee, beans and bacon from the store and pay for such inferior provender by catching and selling fish does not appeal to us at all. We catch fish for our own eating, get all our living by as direct means as possible, that we may be self-sufficient and avoid contributing to the ruthless mechanical system that is destroying the earth.

In this endeavor, no sacrifice is called for, no struggle or effort of will. Such a way is natural. Rather than hardship, it brings peace and inner rewards beyond measure.

Thus shantyboating has become, for us, a point of view, a way of looking at the world and at life. You take neither of them too seriously, nor do you try to understand their complexities. Who can? It is an obviously illogical philosophy, in which the individual is supreme. The claims made on him by his inner beliefs are above the demands of society. He is not without compassion, but his love is expended on those of his fellow men he is in contact with. With no schemes for universal betterment, he tends his own garden.

Is this selfish? No. The selfish man wants more than his share, a higher seat at the table than he is entitled to. One strong enough to stand by himself is not attracted by the prizes which the world offers. He has his own values, receives other rewards, for which there is no competition.

Instead of trying to make everyone alike, the state and society should encourage individualism. Individuals will never be too numerous; in fact, they are becoming harder to find. The river shantyboater has passed away, along with the old river; yet a few renegades will always be found, out in the brush somewhere, or on a forgotten bit of river shore, content with an environment the proud would scorn. The shantyboat strain is not likely to be cultivated out of existence, any more than the earth will ever be completely subdued.

March 27

The bloodroot on the bare hillsides is compensation for the cheerless days of early spring.

17

On many days work continues as long as the light lasts. On this summer evening, however, I am at rest, having done all the work that this day required, and some for which no demand is ever made. Withdrawal from all activity and a thoughtful looking about round out a day, as they do a life, in a manner which harmonizes with the sunset.

Now I look down over the garden, past the gangling locust trees, past the leafy border of the river and over the calm water to the shore and hills beyond, already fading into the cool gray of evening, into the elemental forms of night. The sky still glows with warm light, its colors and formless clouds dimmed by the thick air of stormy June. On the smooth plane of water the only motion is a slight quivering at the edges of the dark reflections.

The evening chorus of birds has diminished, but the wood thrush's full song drifts down the hollow, as if from a celestial region far above. It ceases as the light fades and only the peewee carries on in the silence, his timid whistle expanding and rising into ecstasy, a burst of joy in the face of approaching darkness.

The quiet becomes more intense. Crickets chirp faintly, then a frog down in the creek strums tentative chords and day passes into night.

The song of birds seems to come from open woods and clearings, while the frog has an earthy voice, reminiscent of the primeval wilderness before man's disturbance of it. I try to imagine what these river hills were like when a virgin forest covered them, when there were no farmsteads, meadows and croplands to give diversity to the landscape. I doubt that I could for long be contented and happy alone in the absolute wilderness. I would soon begin to long for a rural countryside—say, what it was seventy-five or a hundred years ago—with the habitations of men in the distance and the effects of their innocent work to be seen here and there.

Even so, I yearn for the wild, I lean toward its absolute solitude, I long to ascend the river to its headwaters in forested mountains, to flow with it down to the sea, the ultimate wilderness.

Today as I swam in the river I looked up with a wild duck's eye into the trees waving as the wind rushed through them, lightly rattling the cottonwood leaves, tossing back the maple branches to reveal their silvery undersides. Above the trees, ragged white clouds sailed across the void of sky.

Suddenly, I felt alone on earth, as I do when lying on the damp ground in spring to see closely the bloodroot raising its leaf sheath through the mold. These moments are not rare. I can summon them when I feel the need to retire into the wilderness. For this is my wilderness, untouched by man, of infinite grace and harmony. Even winter—though its cold may snap the thread of my existence—is part of the gentle, soft-edged creation which is wild nature, ever cheerful and friendly, a solace to the spirit of man.

We live on a frontier and a clear vision can see the wilderness extending into the unknown distance. To keep this view ever before us is not easy. Civilization becomes more clamorous and insistent. It is in a way to dominate the earth. Nature seems already to have lost some of its vitality and health. The river is polluted, the very stars are tampered with. Even in Payne Hollow the situation seems almost hopeless on a Sunday afternoon in summer, when the outboards go skittering over the surface of the river and the hellish sounds come from all quarters. I turn within, let the day pass. Then, early Monday morning, when I go down to the shore, the quiet river seems newly created. Mist lifts from the smooth water, creeps up into Payne Hollow and rises skyward until it catches the light of the morning sun. My faith is renewed, and I rejoice after my own fashion.

AFTERWORD:
THE MEANINGS OF PAYNE HOLLOW

Don Wallis

Harlan Hubbard's *Payne Hollow* abounds with honesty
and modesty and proud joyful moments. Harlan's writing
is exact and true: he never strains for effect, or claims
more (or less) than his due. And so his proud joyful
moments are wonderful and inspire us, sensing as we
do that Harlan means exactly what he says: *My faith is
renewed, and I rejoice after my own fashion.* In this
statement is expressed the triumph of a life.

Harlan's triumph is in his achieving so fully his life's
deepest meaning. In the season he turned twenty-one
years old, he experienced a vision:

> I discovered a truth that seemed to me a revelation.... There
> seemed to be two universes which I termed the world and the
> earth, in either of which I could choose to live. Then I saw
> there was but one, and that I was living on the earth looking
> directly into infinity.

This was Harlan's destiny, his purpose, his need in life.
It meant living in intimate communion with nature: "wild

nature," Harlan writes in *Payne Hollow,* "the gentle, soft-edged creation" that is "a solace to the spirit of man." But the conflict resolved in his vision between "living on the earth" and living in "the world" — the conventional, "civilized" world — was unresolved in his life for more than twenty years, until Harlan was forty-three years old, and newly married to Anna (who was forty-one). Until then Harlan had lived a life partly of the "earth" and partly of "the world." Anna saw his need to break free of the stifling "world" — perhaps she felt her own need to break free — and together they committed themselves to living "a river way of life." Harlan wrote:

> I had no theories to prove. I merely wanted to try living by
> my own hands, independent as far as possible from a system
> of division of labor in which the participant loses most of the
> pleasure of making and growing things for himself. I wanted
> to bring in my own fuel and smell its sweet smoke as it
> burned on the hearth I had made. I wanted to grow my own
> food, catch it in the river, or forage after it. In short, I wanted
> to do as much as I could for myself, because I had already
> realized from partial experience the inexpressible joy of so
> doing.

This was Harlan's entry at last into his envisioned life of "earth" and "infinity." His great achievement was to sustain it for the rest of his life. In the climactic passage of *Payne Hollow*, written when he was seventy-three years old, Harlan is living on the earth looking directly into infinity:

I looked up with a wild duck's eye into the trees waving as the wind rushed through them…. Suddenly I felt alone on earth, as I do when lying on the damp ground in spring to see the bloodroot raising its leaf sheath through the mold. These moments are not rare. I can summon them whenever I feel the need to retire into the wilderness. For this is my wilderness, untouched by man, of infinite grace and harmony.

These moments are not rare. This is one of the essential meanings of *Payne Hollow*.

Another meaning of *Payne Hollow* is embodied in the often-made comparison between Harlan Hubbard and Thoreau. Harlan is said to be a modern-day Thoreau, *Payne Hollow* a modern-day *Walden*. And indeed Thoreau may be said to have made Payne Hollow possible — the place, the life the Hubbards lived there, and the book Harlan wrote about it — for as a young man Harlan read Thoreau and all his life was influenced and inspired by him. Their books bear the same urgent message. Thoreau proclaims it, Harlan murmurs it, but it's the same imperative demand: *Change your life.* Harlan and Thoreau share the same essential wisdom, but there are fateful differences in their lives and work. Harlan settled himself fully at Payne Hollow, and made his home and his living there for the rest of his life, the better part of four decades. Thoreau's stay at Walden Pond lasted two years; then he went back to town. *Walden* is a great work of the inspired imagination; *Payne Hollow* is the real life lived.

"Payne Hollow is our whole life," Harlan wrote in his journal, "the writing and painting just expressions of it." Our *whole* life: all of it, complete, a life wholly lived. The Hubbards gave themselves wholly to Payne Hollow, and they took their living wholly from it; they had everything they wanted and everything they needed, right there: food, shelter, art and music, love and work. It is often ruefully observed that they had to *work* all the time, but I say the Hubbards, rightfully understood, never worked a day in their lives, for their work was their pleasure, task and reward enacted as one: "the inexpressible joy of so doing." And *this* is what the writing and painting are expressions of — the joy of living at Payne Hollow, day-by-day, year-after-year.

Again and again Harlan created, in his art and in his writing, expressions of the river at Payne Hollow, the Payne Hollow woods and the Payne Hollow sky, the house at Payne Hollow in all its weathers and seasons, and often he achieves a poetic depth of truth and beauty, grounded in his careful and intimate relation to the place. In Harlan's eyes Payne Hollow often seems to live a life distinctly and wholly its own, like Harlan's sense of "my wilderness," its nurturing spirit "untouched by man," even by Harlan himself: *The quiet river seems newly created.* This too is one of the meanings of *Payne Hollow.*

The Hubbards, having made their home on their shantyboat for seven epic years, settled at Payne Hollow in the spring of 1952, and there they lived happily ever after, spring of 1952, and there they lived happily ever after, sustaining their "river way of life" to the end. Anna died in May of 1986, at the age of eighty-three. Harlan died in January of 1988, at the age of eighty-eight. Payne Hollow still exists, much as it did when the Hubbards were alive. There has been as yet no rude encroachment of "civilization" upon the elegant and earthy amenities of the place. Books of and on the writing and art of the Hubbards and their lives continue to be published. Visitors still come, many of them searching for something they feel is missing from their lives, some meaning they feel they might find at Payne Hollow. They are looking for the Hubbards; and in a sense they find them, for they are still there at Payne Hollow, in spirit and symbol: their ashes are buried in the earth a few steps from the house, beneath a headstone on which Harlan had a sculptor carve the drawing that is on the dedication page of this book, and is an emblem of their lives:

PUBLISHER'S NOTE

After Harlan Hubbard finished writing *Payne Hollow,* he sent it off to the publisher of his one previous book, *Shantyboat*. It languished there and letters from Harlan seemed to bring little response. This is where Harvey Simmonds (now Brother Benedict) entered the picture. Harvey looked up the Hubbards after he had moved to Covington and was working on the Delta Queen. Harlan told Harvey of his publishing problems and Harvey took it as his mission to solve this. He entered the publisher's office and as Harlan's representative asked for the manuscript back. Their response was that the manuscript had somehow been misplaced and was lost. This was more of a problem than often is the case since there was no copy.

Harvey informed the publisher he was not leaving the premises until the manuscript was found and given to him. After some hours of searching, the manuscript appeared. Without Harvey's persistence you might not be holding the present volume.

Harvey then showed it to Leslie Katz of The Eakins Press, who appreciated it from the outset. Publication was on September 3, 1974. After these copies had been sold, Thomas Y. Crowell published a short-lived edition. Gnomon Press became the book's publisher in 1985.